NO QUARTER

BOUNTY - BOOK ONE

CHRISTINE
D'ABO

D0885385

RIPTIDE
PUBLISHING

Riptide Publishing
PO Box 1537
Burnsville, NC 28714
www.riptidepublishing.com

No Quarter

Cover art: Lou Harper, louharper.com/design.html
Editor: Delphine Dryden, delphinedryden.com/editing
Layout: L.C. Chase, lcchase.com/design.htm

ISBN: 978-1-62649-400-8

Second edition
April, 2016

Also available in ebook:
ISBN: 978-1-62649-399-5

NO QUARTER

BOUNTY - BOOK ONE

CHRISTINE
D'ABO

RIPTIDE
PUBLISHING

TABLE OF
CONTENTS

CHAPTER

ONE

Gar Stitt walked into the Space Jock—the seediest bar on Tybal Station—with a clear head and clear purpose. The stench of vomit, sex, and stale *rymak* beer was enough to turn the stomach of even the most seasoned bounty hunter, but did little to distract Gar from his task. He sidestepped a drunk who was on his way to the floor, blood dripping from his nose where he'd been punched. A Helexian female nearly walked into him, her white hair and tendrils flushing blue with embarrassment before she scurried away.

Careful to avoid getting any of the filth from the bar or its patrons on him, Gar quickly scanned the darkened room for his mark. The mix of colors was muted by the haze in the air. Humans and aliens alike clung haphazardly to the stools and were draped across tables; none were the man he was looking for.

In and out, he'd been promised—in for a quick job and then out to the middle of nowhere for a much-needed break. Gar had already lingered on the station longer than he'd intended, tracking his target. If anyone but Jason Krieg had asked him to take care of the matter, he would have walked away. Six months on various hunts was enough to suck the life out of anyone—Gar was no exception.

He'd been in the Bounty Hunters' Guild long enough that he didn't get stuck with cleanup duties often, so he knew there was something special about this case. Not that Gar could say no to the man who'd given him a renewed sense of purpose after the murder of his family, even if it meant coming to the Space Jock. Jason asked, and Gar jumped. The positive point to the whole thing was a chance to see the infamous Captain Wolf again.

Suppressing a sigh, he focused his attention back on the crowd. For the briefest of seconds, he considered that his reconnaissance report might have misled him. This didn't seem like the captain's normal type of entertainment haven if his file was to be believed. It was too crowded, too exposed, too deep in enemy territory. It went against the pattern, and nothing good happened when normal routines changed.

Fantastic.

Loud, throbbing beats pounded through his body until the fine hairs on the back of his neck stood on end and his brain rattled in his head. He was sure this qualified as music somewhere in the universe, but nowhere *he'd* ever want to visit. What would bring the captain to a hellhole like this? Not that Gar's mark had a particularly discerning reputation, but from the picture in the data file, he thought Wolf would have better taste. Though this was the same man who'd had the balls to waltz into Jason's backyard and try to pull a scam.

Gar would have to cut those balls off.

In the quick lull between songs, a peal of rich, booming laughter from the back room grabbed Gar's attention—the same laugh he'd heard on a vid clip in the data file. Ah, there he was—Captain Faolan Wolf, present and accounted for.

Perhaps this would go more smoothly than he'd first thought. Shifting his weight to loosen his vest and shrug open his long, heavy overcoat, he slid his hand inside to brush the top of the holsters carrying his blasters. His long black blades were secured in special sheaths that would send both knives into his waiting hands with a hard flick of his wrists. They and the leather wrist straps he wore for protection were perfectly hidden from sight within the bulk of his coat.

With any luck, he would dispose of the infamous captain and be back on the *Geilt* in time for his meal.

A wall of silence fell over the bar as Gar walked past. While he rarely frequented Tybal Station as he had in his youth, his reputation remained firmly in place. He ignored hooded stares, taking silent pleasure in how at least half the people averted their gazes in an attempt to escape his notice. Those who didn't were probably looking for some excitement. They might get their wish if things didn't go the way he intended tonight.

It was Gar's appearance that helped him blend into a crowd—until he unleashed his special brand of judgment. Then, of course, those who survived had his image burned into their memory: jacket, black vest, crisp white shirt. He looked to be on his way to a sophisticated social function on one of the Earth colonies, not frequenting the bowels of a hellhole like Tybal.

Gar had long since become accustomed to hell. It suited him.

The crowd parted, making it easier for him to avoid the layer of scum that clung to everything and everyone in the place. When he reached the back room, the captain's voice slipped from the half-shut door. Two rather bulky men flanked the entrance, large, meaty arms crossed over their chests. Gar laced his hands behind his back and let his gaze slide from the man on the left to the one on the right. Their clubbed fists would easily crack his jaw, but he doubted it would come to a single blow. Cocking a lean eyebrow, he waited.

It didn't take long for the man on the left to squirm.

"Private party," the behemoth slurred.

Gar snorted.

"The captain doesn't want to be disturbed," the one on the right bit out, a little more coherent than his mate.

Bowing his head toward the man, Gar took a half step closer. He didn't raise his voice, despite the resurgence of the blaring music. No, he kept it even, his words clipped and clear.

"Open the door."

"Why the fuck should we listen to you?" the guard on the right spat, pushing his face into Gar's as he did.

Gar jabbed his thumb into the side of the man's throat, collapsing him to the floor, gasping and coughing. The movement was so fast the other bouncer barely had time to blink before Gar returned his hands to their original position behind his back. Raising his eyebrow again, he waited for the remaining man to push the door all the way open.

Gar spoke softly as he stepped over the moaning man. "He'll need medical attention. You might want to see to it immediately."

In the back room, a red haze hung high in the air, the sweet scent telling him that it was most likely an erotigen. Great, now he was going to have a hard-on for a week. He stepped fully into the room and waited for someone to notice his presence.

It took longer than expected.

Captain Wolf lay on a large, thick pallet that covered most of the floor. He was barefoot, wearing only a pair of black leather pants and a rich-green military jacket that gaped open. His bare chest and stomach were partially covered by the long hair of a woman currently fighting with a young, attractive man for the privilege of sucking the captain's cock. His wide grin exposed a mouth full of perfect white teeth, and amusement made his eyes sparkle.

"Now, Jona, you must learn to share. There's more than enough of me to go around and Ziva has been more than patient."

The cooing and moaning of the pair would have been funny under different circumstances. For that matter, the impressive size of the captain's cock would have been a matter of interest. Gar knew the only thing it rivaled was the size of the man's ego.

His slow gaze moved up Wolf's body and over his chest, taking in the long brown hair that reached the top of his shoulders, and finally coming to rest on his startling blue gaze. It took all Gar's years of training to keep his surprise from showing. He'd only laid eyes on the captain once before, during a time when he'd been in no position to draw attention to himself or his actions. Now, subjected to Wolf's piercing inspection, long-buried feelings of uncertainty and inexperience rose.

The captain's amusement never wavered, even as he pulled Jona's mouth from his straining cock and leaned forward to stage-whisper in his ear. "It seems we have company."

"Captain Wolf."

"Ooh, now that is an accent I haven't heard in a very long time. Damasmus? No, too refined for there. Zeten?" He shifted his weight to one hip, attempting to look around Gar. "Can't see the stick up your ass, but it must be there."

"Stand up."

"I'd much rather you lie down. Take that jacket off. Maybe your pants. I'll look for the stick."

The pair on either side of Wolf snickered, the woman turning her head to lick his nipple. The captain gazed down at her and placed a kiss on her forehead. Gar didn't look away, but knew he was being tested—the captain was trying to catch him off guard.

"Look, I don't mind sharing. She's quite good."

Gar let out a soft sigh, but the captain's hearing was too good.

"Not interested. Sorry, Ziva, I don't think you're his type. Jona's exceptional, but you might be a bit rough for him. Don't know if I can allow that."

"You've been playing in the wrong backyard, pirate. You should have known you'd never make it out of Krieg's territory untouched."

Wolf grinned and let his gaze travel lazily down Gar's body, lingering on his groin before meeting his eyes again with a wink. "Definitely from Zeten. Damn, I forgot how sexy that accent was."

Impatience poked at Gar, but he refused to react. Narrowing his eyes, he took a half step forward and dropped his hands to his sides. The motion caused his overcoat to pull, none too subtly revealing the butts of his blasters. The captain had a reputation for liking things rough—Gar was more than happy to accommodate.

He knew the second Ziva and Jona spied his weapons. They rolled away from Wolf, snatching their clothing as they went. Without another word, they ran naked from the room. The captain actually pouted at the loss of his companions, watching after them as they scurried away.

"That wasn't nice. Now I'm left all alone with a stiff cock and no one to relieve it."

"You should have thought of that before vacationing on Tybal."

"I like you, bounty hunter." He pushed his cock back into his pants and hauled himself to his feet. "So, how much am I worth these days?"

Of course the size of the bounty made a difference to a man like Captain Wolf. This time Gar couldn't hold back the eye roll, eliciting a chuckle from Wolf.

"Come on, my reputation is at stake. How much?"

"Two million."

"Excellent. That last job must have bumped me up a level."

He slid the green coat from his body, putting Gar face-to-face with the most perfectly sculpted bare chest and arms he'd seen in ages. A beautifully intricate tattoo of a *cyrax* dragon on his left arm rippled as he reached down, grabbed a tight-fitting shirt, and pulled it on. Somehow, the man looked even better clad in the clingy fabric than he had half-naked.

Giving his head a slight shake, Gar refocused on the matter at hand. The captain caught the small motion, and his grin widened.

"It's the erotigen, bounty hunter. Making you all hot and bothered, isn't it?"

How Gar had forgotten about the red haze, he wasn't sure, but the bastard was probably right. His cock was noticeably harder than a moment ago, the blood pounding through it echoed by the pounding in his head. It also explained why the sight of the captain pulling on a pair of knee-high boots was the most arousing thing he'd witnessed in years. Not that Gar was particularly attracted to men—sex was more of a way to take the edge off than anything else. It didn't really matter if his partner was male or female, as long as they didn't talk and left him alone afterward.

He had to admit, the idea of sex with Captain Wolf was strangely appealing at the moment.

Giving his head another shake, he let his annoyance slip through as he pulled out a blaster and pointed it at his mark. Time to put an end to this little game.

"Let's go, Captain Wolf."

"Faolan. With you looking all dark and sexy like that, you can call me Faolan."

The name suited him. So did the military jacket and sword belt that he fastened around his hips. Wolf slid the sheathed weapon itself across the floor, and Gar picked it up with one hand, shoving it into the back of his own belt, where it hung awkwardly under his coat. Even without the sword, a fully dressed Captain Wolf—Faolan—was a force to be reckoned with. He suddenly looked a lot more dangerous than he had moments earlier.

Flexing his fingers on the butt and trigger of his weapon, Gar let out a slow, even breath and leveled the laser sight on Faolan's chest.

"Time to go . . . *Captain*."

Faolan took a step closer, and Gar realized the man was slightly taller and leaner than he was. He adjusted his stance in anticipation of an attack. The action caught the captain's attention, and he lifted his chin slightly.

"Itching for a fight, bounty hunter? 'Cause I'm fucking hard as hell and unless you're going to bend over so I can bury myself in your sweet ass, I'm just as happy to beat the shit out of you."

"I'd like to see you try."

Not normally so easily goaded, Gar mentally hit himself for taking the bait. Even the captain seemed surprised—momentary shock melting into amused interest. Another step had Faolan's chest pressed firmly against the barrel of the blaster, but he seemed oblivious to it.

Deep blue eyes locked onto Gar's, Faolan reached up and ran his thumb along Gar's goatee.

"Now this is sexy. I haven't had a man with facial hair suck my cock in a long time. Though it would be a shame to fill your mouth too long. I wouldn't be able to hear you moan with that wonderful accent." His finger slid from Gar's chin to brush his jawline. "Are you sure you don't want to fuck?"

Gar's cock twitched at the suggestion. He knew Faolan would be a good lover—could tell by the intensity of his gaze, the gentleness of his touch. Despite the temptation and the pull of the erotigen, Gar's sense of duty to Jason was stronger. Thumbing the blaster up to the next setting, he cocked an eyebrow.

"Quite."

With a deep sigh and a slight pout, Faolan shrugged. "Best we're off, then. Through the bar or out the back door?"

The heavy stress on "back door" elicited another eye roll before Gar dipped his head toward the bar entrance. "Move."

"We need to work on your conversational skills, bounty hunter. These one-word responses are already getting boring."

"I wouldn't want the sound of my voice to get you overexcited. That way."

Chuckling, Faolan walked past him into the crowd, one hand automatically resting where the hilt of his sword would have been. Gar's prisoner flirted with everything on two or more legs as he led his captor out of the Space Jock. He even went so far as to run his hand down the feathered back of one of the waitresses.

"Stitt's bringing in the captain," someone hissed as they shuffled past.

"He's dead," another agreed.

"But I'll leave a fucking *gorgeous* corpse." Faolan winked at them before leaning in, kissing one of the barmaids on the mouth and stepping out the door.

Out on the streets, Gar kept his guard up. He doubted the captain was there alone, and it was likely Wolf's crew had been alerted to his plight. Gar needed to get him out of sight and off planet as quickly as possible. He'd deal with the crew only once their leader was taken care of.

Pushing Faolan against the damp stone wall of the dark alley outside the bar, he roughly jerked the captain's hands behind his back and into a set of electro-cuffs. This section of the station was close to ruin from years of meteorite showers and high acid rain. The depressing conditions did little to dampen Faolan's vivacious attitude. He even laughed as Gar flipped him around so they were face-to-face.

"God, I bet you have all sorts of cool shit we could use in bed. A little heavy bondage. I bet you'd get off on being the mark for once."

"If you want to see my gag, keep it up with the smart mouth." Gar pressed his com unit and waited for the connection. "It's Stitt. I need a cell and a route cleared."

Faolan's gaze narrowed, giving Gar the impression that he was making a quick decision. Whatever it was, it didn't take him long to come to some sort of conclusion. He licked his lips, his smile slipping back into place.

"Before you and Krieg throw away the key on me, aren't you the least bit curious to know why a man with a bounty as large as the one I have on my head showed up on your doorstep? Because, really, stupidity wasn't in my character profile."

"One moment please, Jason." Gar tapped his com unit again and waited.

Faolan licked his lips again. "While I might be cocky, I'm not an idiot. We raided an Earth Loyalist cruiser a month ago and came across something . . . interesting. Considering your boss's reputation, I thought he might be curious to see what the new radicals were trying to smuggle home. He refused to take my calls, so this was the fastest way to get his attention."

Impatience wasn't something Gar normally battled with, but Faolan seemed to have the unique ability to test his control. Pressing the barrel of the blaster into the side of the captain's neck, Gar waited for him to continue.

Instead of showing fear, Faolan simply seemed amused. "I'm not going to tell you unless you ask nicely."

Leaning his weight into the blaster, Gar shifted his face so it was only a few inches away from Faolan's.

"Please."

Faolan sighed, his eyes dipping shut for a moment before he returned his gaze to Gar's.

"Someday I'm going to make you beg just so I can hear you say that again."

"If you don't start talking, you're not going to live past the next thirty seconds."

Faolan slid forward so the tip of his nose brushed Gar's, and lowered his voice so it barely reached him even in the confines of the alley.

"We found what I thought was nothing more than some trinkets, a bit of jewelry some Loyalist whore might miss when the ship disappeared. Turns out, there was something a bit more valuable hidden in plain sight. A precious stone the size of an energy capacitor."

"And why should I care?"

Faolan's breath tickled Gar's neck. The aroma of musk, erotigen, and hydro vodka clung to the pirate like a second skin. Gar's cock twitched again at the scent.

"You should care, *Gar* Stitt, because the stone gives its holder the ability to read another's thoughts."

Everything around Gar seemed to narrow. Aside from his blaster pressed against Faolan's chin and the captain's hands locked behind his back in the electro-cuffs, the rest of their bodies was pressed firmly together.

They were nearly the same height, and their swollen cocks rocked against each other through the fabric of their clothing. The pressure was pleasant, more enticing because of the erotigen. Strangely, Gar knew if he were to release Faolan's hands, he could easily relax into his embrace.

Instead of giving in to the temptation, he reached up and tapped his com unit. "Did you get that, sir?" He listened to his instructions, keeping his gaze locked on the amused expression of the pirate. Jason changed his orders, and Gar nodded, despite the fact no one but Faolan could see him. "Of course I'm sure. I'll report back once I have it."

Faolan looked surprised as Gar leaned in and disengaged the lock on the cuffs, then pulled the sword from his belt and handed it over. Wolf slid it back into place by feel, never taking his eyes off Gar. "I assume this means your boss is interested in what I'm selling."

"My boss wants me to check out the stone. See if it does what you claim. If so . . . I'm authorized to make arrangements to obtain it."

"And if your boss doesn't give me the price I want? Half the galaxy would kill for this thing."

"Half the galaxy can't remove the bounty from your head and set you up with enough credits to last a lifetime."

Faolan nodded once. "Fair enough. I need to take you to my ship."

"Lead the way."

Gar stepped back to let him by, but the pirate had other ideas. With unexpected speed and grace, Faolan grabbed him by the wrist and spun him around. Now his back was against the alley wall. Pinning him in place, Faolan thrust his knee between Gar's and pressed the top of his thigh against Gar's balls and shaft. Instead of attacking, Faolan crushed his mouth against Gar's. Faolan's tongue pressed inward, invading his mouth with the taste of vodka and the promise of pleasure. The blaster Gar still held fell lifeless to the ground. Large hands roamed Gar's chest, fingers forced their way under his overcoat and vest, only to be thwarted by his shirt. Faolan let out a low growl and broke the kiss with a gasp.

"You wear too many clothes, Stitt."

"And I'm still armed."

With a flick of his wrist, the long black knife sprang from its sheath, the handle landing smoothly in the palm of his waiting hand. Gar pressed the blade to Faolan's throat and cocked an eyebrow in question. Good kisser or not, Gar wouldn't hesitate to kill the captain where he stood. Faolan recognized this, but didn't seem intimidated by Gar's ruthlessness.

"Definitely too many clothes. We need to work on that."

"Your ship?"

Faolan brushed his lips softly over Gar's once more before stepping away. "Well, you see, I'm going to need your help there."

For the love of all that's good, why did he make things so difficult?

"Mutiny, Captain?"

Definitely the wrong thing to say. Faolan straightened to his full height, lowering his chin to look down his nose at Gar. His shoulder-length brown hair swept forward, framing his face and partially covering his eyes. In the blink of an eye, Faolan changed from devil-may-care pirate to deadly adversary.

"I trust my crew with my life, and they trust me with theirs. Mutiny is the last thing I'm worried about."

It was the first serious thing Wolf had said since Gar walked through the door of the bar's back room. "Then why would you need my assistance?"

"I didn't want to risk the ship or my crew by landing on the station. I couldn't trust your boss not to kill me on sight for invading his pleasure port. They dropped me off. I'm to meet them in three days at a specified rendezvous four light jumps from here." Leaning forward, he winked at Gar. "Fancy a trip?"

If *anyone* but Jason had asked him to take on this assignment, he would have walked away, wanting no part of the man in front of him or the trouble he was sure to bring. Instead, Gar tucked his knife back into its sheath and pushed his blaster back into the holster. Straightening his vest and pulling his overcoat closed so the hem brushed the top of his boots, he spun on his heel and stalked out of the alley in the direction of the landing docks.

Faolan silently fell into step beside him. Gar was irritated to see the man was grinning. No, this wasn't going to be a pleasant experience. He forced his body to relax so he could at least stop grinding his teeth long enough to lay down the law. He rarely brought anyone on board the *Geilt* unless they were bound, gagged, and in a cage. Or as a corpse. Guests were an anomaly.

"There are rules I expect you to follow. If you get out of line, I'll kill you."

Faolan chuckled. "Oh, this is going to be fun."

CHAPTER

TWO

"Why am I not surprised?" Faolan fixed a smirk on his face and followed Stitt onto the ship.

He'd often said you could tell someone's personality from their living quarters. The *Geilt* was exactly what Faolan expected—sterile and cold. Sliding a hand along the side wall, he took in as much of the room as he could. Triple security circuits on the hatch, reinforced hull, laser rifle by the door to the cabin, compact food replicator along the back wall. All practical and boring. What the hell did a man like Stitt spend his credits on if not comforts for his ship? It certainly wasn't alcohol or whores, if his reputation was anything to go by.

He should have listened to Mace and brought his personal pleasure mod for entertainment. God, this was going to be duller than he'd anticipated.

Still, he was flattered Krieg sent Gar after him. Faolan had worked hard to earn the reputation of being a dangerous bastard, and would have been insulted if someone with a lesser reputation had been ordered to collect him. The last thing he wanted was to be discounted as a hack or has-been, not worthy of a better hunter. Gar was the best out there.

Too bad he seemed frigid.

"So, what do you do for fun around these parts?" Faolan grinned, making a show of it as he ran a fingertip over the top of a shelf, only to inspect it for nonexistent dust.

Gar glared at him from over his shoulder, still heading to the couch. "Deal with criminals like you."

The bounty hunter's movements were fluid as he rolled his shoulders and slipped the heavy overcoat down his arms to reveal a formfitting jacket and ass-hugging trousers. Faolan was more than happy to ogle that sight until Gar turned back around and cleared his throat, forcing Faolan's gaze to his face. Gar's irritation was clear by the single lift of his eyebrow. How could one man say so much with such a minimal effort?

Faolan shrugged. "I was thinking about asses and wanted to check yours out."

"I'd prefer if you didn't."

Touchy bastard. "I'll take it under advisement."

"You want to take off your jacket?" Mock civility oozed from Gar.

"Is that an invitation for me to get naked, pretty boy? I'm more than happy to oblige." Faolan ignored the twitching of his still-hard cock at the thought of getting Gar into bed. Or against the wall . . . or on the floor. The damn erotigen was still working overtime, short-circuiting his brain when he should be strategizing. *Shit.* Rookie mistake to have let Ziva use that crap.

Gar didn't even crack a smile. Faolan slipped the heavy coat down his arms. He tossed it in the direction of the black sofa, trying not to laugh at the horrified expression on Gar's face as it sailed through the air and landed in a heap at the edge of the couch. With a shake of his head, Gar turned and laced his hands behind his back, his gaze locked on the offending clothing now littering his ship.

"I mentioned there were some rules." With a sigh, he walked toward the jacket Faolan had just thrown. Bending slightly at the waist as though the action might wrinkle his perfectly pressed dark suit, he picked it up. Holding it out from his body, he clicked his tongue. "The first is: don't mess up my ship."

"Can I mess you up instead?" The words flew from Faolan's mouth before he could think to stop them. Not that he would take them back. He really did need to fuck something.

Gar stared at him hard. He noticed the change in the other man— the darkening of his eyes and the bob of his throat as he swallowed. With Gar's overcoat gone and his jacket open, it was also easier to see the bulge in the front of his pants. It would be simple enough to blame the erotigen, but the drug would only do so much. There was something in the way Gar moved, shifting to gently drape Faolan's jacket over the back of the couch, that told him the hunter was trying to fight the effects of both the drugs and Faolan's words. It didn't look like Gar was winning. Unresolved lust burned through Faolan's body, making his balls tighten and his cock leak. If he didn't fuck something soon, he really *would* kill someone.

Gar's voice shook him out of his musings. "Rule number two. While you're on my ship, I'm in charge. No games, no deceit. I expect the total truth the entire time or else I turn around and deliver your ass to Krieg."

Faolan snorted. "I won't promise you that."

"Then this trip is over now."

Gar marched in the direction of his overcoat, and Faolan *knew* he was going for the electro-cuffs. Reaching out, Faolan gripped Gar's arm, stopping him where he stood before pulling him close. "Hey, settle down."

"Don't push your luck, *Captain.*"

"I'm not. I can promise you the truth, but *no one* is in charge of me. Understand?"

He kept his eyes locked on Gar's, but suddenly found it hard to concentrate. Heat radiated from Gar in waves, enticing him, inviting him to lean in. Damn it, he needed to keep a clear head if he was going to pull this off and get his crew out of their current mess. Krieg's money was the answer to so many problems—all he had to do was keep his cock under control and win the confidence of the man in front of him.

Gar's blue gaze roamed over his face. Faolan barely managed to suppress a shiver. He wet his bottom lip with his tongue, and did it again when Gar's attention slipped down to watch.

"Any other rules I need to be aware of?" He flexed his fingers on Gar's biceps, testing the firmness of the muscle beneath the layers of fabric.

Faolan had never found strong men to be overly attractive. He liked to be the one on top—especially if his partner was younger. Gar was an interesting mix of old-galaxy manners and youthful vibrancy, even if he hid it beneath a mask of ice. What fun Faolan could have chipping away at the layers. Who would he find hiding under the surface?

Gar jerked his arm free and took a step back. The distance, while not great, gave them both room to breathe. Faolan watched as the hunter pulled the hem of his jacket down, as if to straighten invisible wrinkles. Nervous tic? Didn't seem likely, but he stored it away for further observation.

"Rule number three," Gar continued, clearing his throat. "Do what you like in this room, but the rest of the ship is off-limits."

"Have some cargo you're scared I might want to sneak a peek at?"

"This is my home. Respect it." Gar turned his face away, gaze drifting in the direction of a door off to the side.

Faolan found himself nodding. "Respect is earned, not granted on a demand."

The words hit home with Gar. Faolan could see by the tightening of his mouth and the briefly squinting eyes. Whatever he was feeling, the fleeting emotion was crushed, and his impassive mask fell back into place. Quite possibly, Faolan had finally met someone more fucked up than himself.

Gar crossed his arms and huffed. "Enough of this. What are the coordinates to your ship? I'd like to get there as quickly as possible. *If* your crew can be trusted to do what you told them, I want to be ready early."

Anger flashed through him, along with the urge to punch Gar. "My crew is loyal to me. You'd do well to remember that."

Faolan had fought long and hard to earn the respect of every man and woman on his ship. They worked, fought, and loved like a family. He'd happily die for each and every one of them if called upon to do so—and he knew the feeling was mutual. What right did this loner have to even *pretend* to criticize them?

Before he could stop himself, he closed the distance between them and pressed into Gar's personal space. "We go nowhere until I'm confident they won't be harmed. I don't trust you not to betray me."

"And I don't trust you not to shoot me in the back. So we're on mutual ground."

Seconds ticked off in Faolan's head as he memorized the expression on Gar's face. He'd dealt with men like this hunter before, and knew if there was some deeper emotion, it would be ugly. Like the men who'd chased him down, taken his wife from him, and left him in his current state. A snort escaped him before he could stop it.

Gar lifted his eyebrow. "What?"

"You think you're something special. Don't you?"

Gar didn't respond, which only served to piss Faolan off more. No, he couldn't lose control of the situation now, not with so much at stake. Twisting his anger into cocky bravado, he grinned wide enough to show all his teeth, in an attempt to turn the tables from confrontation into something else.

"Hunter, you think because you live in Krieg's back pocket that you have control of everything and everyone in this sector. If you were to snap your fingers, you could have whatever you want laid out before you. But do you know what? You're wrong. My crew will be at the coordinates. We have three days to kill in the meantime. It's your call on how we do it."

Gar didn't look away—his pale-blue irises were unrelenting in their appraisal. It would have been unnerving if it weren't for the thinly veiled lust showing through the man's mask.

Faolan shouldn't have been surprised when Gar took a step back, visibly swallowed, and shifted his gaze to the cockpit door.

"I need to maneuver the ship into the queue for planetary takeoff. Stay here."

Faolan bowed deep at the waist, holding his arms out wide. "Of course."

"Fucker." Gar turned sharply before he marched into the cockpit, the door automatically sliding closed behind him.

The air in the room felt thin as Faolan took several breaths to calm his racing heart. *Gods-damned erotigen.* He'd have to play this one fast and loose, try to keep Gar off-balance until he could get back to his ship. Mace would be able to pull something up on the bastard at that point. She had a way of digging out the dirt in a person's life, no matter how deeply they thought it was buried. And if she couldn't . . . well, she could always make something up.

Hooking his thumbs into the waistband of his pants, he sauntered around the room. There had to be something on this ship he could use against Gar to ensure things went the way he wanted.

He wasn't surprised to find the door to the cockpit locked when he tried it. It proved that despite being dosed with drugs, Gar could still think straight. Good to know. Faolan wanted a challenge, not some pushover.

The only other door in the room, aside from the exit, was also locked, this time with a bio scanner and voiceprint identifier. Gar apparently took no chances when it came to his ship's security. Not that it would stop Faolan from cracking it when he needed to, but it would take longer than usual. Curiosity gnawed at his insides. Gar was proving to be more of a mystery and a challenge than he'd anticipated. A grin slipped onto his face as he continued to inspect the room.

The couch took up a large part of the area, and there were very few personal effects decorating the walls. A computer terminal along the side wall was also locked down with bio access. Casting a quick glance over his shoulder at the cockpit door, he slipped into the terminal chair and began running through several of his tried-and-tested hacking techniques. The screen flashed red with each failed attempt, escalating his annoyance. Bastard bounty hunter was good—which pissed him off more. There had to be something else.

Spinning the seat around, he looked at the room again, this time with an eye for anything out of the ordinary. Gar was a loner, apparently had no addictions, and lived a minimalistic life if the rest of the ship was anything like this room. The boy needed to have some fun! Faolan couldn't have lived like this—he'd die from the monotony of it all. Fucking, fighting, and flying his ship were what ruled his current life. Mix in raids on Loyalist ships and colonies and he had everything a man with no future could ever want.

As the minutes passed, he grew almost resolved to not finding out Gar's secret—because everyone had at least one—before the hunter came back. But when his gaze landed on the silver panel alongside the computer terminal, he knew he'd found what he was looking for.

Something unusual.

He dropped to his knees as he pulled out a black-bladed knife from his boot. The panel fell away surprisingly easy given the nature of Gar's security protocols. What Faolan wasn't expecting to see was an old-fashioned safe embedded in the wall. No bio scanner, just a mechanical spin dial combination. Honestly, the idea was brilliant.

Most criminals wouldn't have a clue how the combination lock worked, let alone how to get past it.

Thankfully, he wasn't the average criminal.

Cracking his fingers, he leaned in until his ear rested just above the dial. He knew the basic principle of the thing—turn the dial until you hit the correct number, then go in the opposite direction. Simple. However, the sheer number of numeric combinations would drive away most people.

Setting the dial to start at zero, he closed his eyes and listened for the steady clicking of the locking mechanism. He, like many of his race, had exceptional hearing, so he was able to recognize the louder snap of the barrel when he hit the right number. Grinning, he reversed the dial's direction. It took only a few minutes more to find the other numbers. Leaning back, he took a deep breath before cracking the rusty metal door open.

His smile quickly morphed into a scowl as he peered inside, not quite sure what he was looking at. Devoid of anything precious like credits, drugs, or weapons, the safe seemed to contain only an old personal picture display unit and a small metal object. Ignoring the display unit, he snatched the other item and rose to his feet.

A watch?

The metal was pitted and discolored along the back and strap. The glass of the face was worn, giving it a fogged appearance. The second hand wasn't moving; instead it stood at attention pointing straight up. Wait . . . no, it wasn't a second hand. No other hand existed, which confused the hell out of him. What good was a watch you couldn't tell time with? For that matter, what good was a watch based on a planetary solar cycle when you lived on a spaceship?

He flipped it over and around in his hand, wondering about the history of the thing. What the hell was a bounty hunter doing with something as antiquated as this anyway?

Faolan didn't notice the blade of Gar's knife until it was pressed firmly against his throat, the edge digging deep enough to draw blood.

"What the . . . *fuck* are you doing?" Gar's voice was little more than a hiss against his ear.

"I got bored."

"Give it to me." Gar held his free hand out, waiting to collect the object.

"What the hell is it?" Faolan moved slowly, knowing he'd really pushed his luck this time. "Looks like a watch."

"*Now*."

Gar's fingers wrapped around the metal the moment Faolan released it. Only then did Gar ease the pressure of the blade from against his neck, allowing him to breathe easier.

"Touchy." He pressed his fingers against the wound to check how deep he'd been cut. He'd live.

Gar ignored him. Dropping to his knees, he carefully set the object back inside the safe. Before closing the door, he pressed several buttons on the inside.

"It won't work, you know." Faolan knew exactly what Gar had just done. "It will only take me another few minutes to crack the new code, and I'll be right back inside."

The short bark of laughter that escaped him died when Gar spun him around and slammed his body against the wall. The air fled his lungs, making his head spin. When he was once again able to focus his vision, Gar was panting just as hard, both lust and rage contorting his boyish looks.

"I told you the rules. No touching my stuff. Show me respect and I'll show you the same."

"And I told you respect has to be earned. What the hell was that thing?"

Gar didn't respond right away. Faolan couldn't help but notice the bulge in the hunter's pants. Faolan's cock, still half-hard from earlier, leaped to full attention at the realization Gar was still fiercely aroused. Gar's gaze hardened with an intensity that made Faolan writhe in place, but he finally growled out an answer.

"It's a . . . stopwatch. Tells you how long a task takes you. It was my father's."

The remorse with which he said the last told Faolan there was more to the story. Still, he considered himself a smart man, and knew now was not the time to push for answers.

Now was most certainly the time for fucking.

He shifted his thigh against Gar's cock and leaned in close. "So now your precious stopwatch is put away and you have me at your mercy, what are you going to do?"

"Kill you."

A cold and in control Gar was sexy, but having him angry and aroused, poised on the edge of that same control, was fucking *hot*.

Faolan leaned forward and licked the shell of Gar's ear. "I don't think so. Despite me having pissed you off, you're intrigued by the trinket I have on my ship." Another swirl of his tongue against the hot skin. "Plus I don't think you'd want to disappoint Krieg."

"I'll just kill you and hunt your ship down. Save me the headache."

Faolan knew he shouldn't laugh, but he couldn't help it. "You'll never track them down without the coordinates." Tugging his hand free, he dug into the pocket of his pants and pulled out a small gold disk. "Which are safely on here."

As expected, Gar tried to grab the disk out of Faolan's grasp, but he was too slow. He stumbled back a step or two before regaining his balance. "Give it to me."

"Wouldn't do you any good. It has a security code on it. Good luck trying to crack it too. It requires the code to be spoken in my voice and, of course, I've built in a safeguard. I say the wrong thing and you're flying into a sun."

Gar closed his eyes. "Fuck."

"I'm no novice when it comes to these things, hunter. You should have known that from the start."

Gar gave his head a slight shake before straightening. "We'll be at the dimension gate soon. I need those coordinates."

Lust rolled through Faolan, an all-encompassing burn growing in strength with every look he cast on Gar. He wanted this man—now. Holding the disk out between them, he thrust his hip out to the side and grinned.

"You want it? Come and get it."

CHAPTER

THREE

Gar was about to explode. His head pounded from the erotigen and the frustration of having the pain-in-the-ass captain on his ship. The guy had gone into his safe and touched his father's stopwatch—Gar's one special personal possession, the only thing he gave a damn about.

This was why he hated cleanup jobs—they never went the way he wanted. Give him a simple catch and retrieve or a kill any day. If Faolan became too much more of an issue, that was exactly what he'd turn this into—a kill.

"Well?" Faolan taunted him with a bright grin, waving the disk at him with short, quick motions.

He'd set the ship on autopilot to the dimension gate, where it would hold until he gave it the next coordinates. It would take at least thirty minutes to get there, but he wasn't in the mood for games. Especially since his body wasn't completely his own at the moment.

He never did drugs. Hardly ever drank. The idea of losing control scared the shit out of him, and to have that sucked away by artificial means? Well, he wouldn't do it to himself. Unfortunately, when something like an erotigen entered his system, leading a clean lifestyle wasn't an advantage. It had hit him harder than it would an experienced user, lingering in his body longer.

Making him horny as hell.

Closing his eyes, he tried to catch his breath. Anger and desire mixed inside his body, pushing him to the edge. Seeing Faolan with his father's stopwatch in his hand had been enough to make him see red, throwing him off-balance. Another wave of dizziness hit him, sending his body lunging to the side.

"Whoa there."

Firm hands were on his biceps, holding him still. That musk, rich and heady, was back. He sucked in a breath, pulling Faolan's scent into his lungs. One of Faolan's large hands snaked around him to press against his lower back, while the other began to work the buttons of his waistcoat.

"I think you've gotten yourself overexcited, hunter."

He shivered. Faolan's deep voice was steady, and as always it sounded one step away from a laugh. Mentally, he latched on to it, hoping it would bring him back from the hell he was slipping into.

"The drug." He shook his head and swallowed. "Can't think."

"I didn't really believe the pure image you'd always put out there, hunter. Figured a man like you would . . . indulge. Even if you didn't like to advertise the fact."

He let Faolan lead him to the couch and pull him down so they were practically on top of each other. The outside of their thighs pressed together firmly, the intimacy of contact sending another shiver through him. Sitting helped, let him catch his breath and regain at least a small part of his composure. Faolan leaned close, his lips against Gar's ear.

"When you got angry, it increased your heart rate and sent the erotigen coursing through that very hot body of yours."

Looking down, he saw Faolan had managed to pull his waistcoat open, leaving his shirt the only barrier. He shifted his gaze to meet blue eyes that said more than words ever could. Faolan's long brown hair had slipped forward again, and Gar actually half lifted his hand to push the strands behind the other man's ear. He stopped in time, but not before the captain noticed.

"You want to touch me, hunter? Go ahead. I don't bite. Not on the first date at least."

"No."

The word was from his lips before he even considered it. Faolan chuckled, playing with a button on his shirt.

"There is a natural antidote for the drug. Endorphins. The best way to release them is from sex."

"Or I could just beat the hell out of you." Or beat off a few times. But he'd have to secure Faolan first to keep him out of trouble. With the drug zinging through his veins, it seemed like an impossible amount of effort, especially when he had a more-than-willing partner in front of him.

Faolan wasn't making things any easier. "Sounds like we're back to where we started this evening. I'd still rather fuck you."

He rolled his eyes closed and imagined what it would feel like to have Faolan bent over him, what it would feel like to have Faolan's cock sliding in and out of his body. He bit his lower lip to keep the moan trapped inside. The noise seemed to encourage Faolan, and his fingers picked up speed as he worked the buttons free.

"Hunter, it's my fault you're in this state. Seeing as we're going to be working together for a little while, I feel it's my responsibility to help you out. Prove to you I'm a good partner for this little adventure of ours."

"I'll never trust you."

"I don't need your trust. Not yet anyway."

And he didn't need Faolan's, either, not for this. Not if they kept it quick, functional, and uncomplicated. The cool air tickled his chest as inch by inch of his skin was revealed. Faolan's fingertips caressed the muscles over his stomach, and Gar couldn't help but watch the pirate's face, see the appreciative looks as he continued to strip Gar's clothes from him.

"I knew you were hiding one fucking hot body under all this shit. Take it off. I want to see you."

Shifting, he let Faolan pull the waistcoat off and didn't even blink when it fell to the floor. The only thing remaining was his half-unbuttoned shirt, which was gone in another moment as well, leaving him bare from the waist up with the exception of his knives and wrist straps.

Faolan let out a low whistle as he ran his hands over the sheaths strapped to Gar's forearms. The black blades blended in with the leather, secretive and deadly.

"These are even more impressive like this. Where did you get them?"

"My own creation."

"They're stunning. Just like you, hunter."

With swift, sure fingers, Faolan undid the buckles holding the straps on first one, then the other of Gar's arms. The blades fell to the floor with a *thunk*, leaving Gar's skin exposed and sensitive.

Faolan pressed him back against the couch until he was lying nearly all the way flat. While he wasn't as broad as Faolan, he was in good shape. He knew the appeal of his body, even if he rarely took advantage of the pleasure others offered him.

Bending his head over Gar's stomach, Faolan placed a kiss just above the belly button. The gentle contact shot straight to Gar's cock, and arched his back. Faolan chuckled, licking a circle around the hole.

"Smooth skin. I like that."

"And if it wasn't smooth?"

"I'd like that too."

Gar should have been jolted to reality by the admission, but he wasn't. Faolan would fuck anything—that much was clear. Gar wasn't the type of man to simply allow himself to be used by another—man, woman, or alien.

Control—he needed to regain it before things went too far.

Letting out a loud growl, he pushed Faolan hard, sending him flying backward into a half sprawl. Faolan didn't move; instead, he grinned at Gar with that wide smile of his.

"Do you have a bed in this ship or do you want to do this right here?"

Gar's body burned. He couldn't fight the drug any longer, and from the look on Faolan's face, he wouldn't have to. "You haven't earned the privilege of my bed."

Gar shuddered as he crawled along the couch, covering the captain's body with his own.

"When you're horny, your accent gets stronger. It's a real turn-on."

He held himself over Faolan. The erotigen might have been the catalyst, but it wasn't the cause of the fire burning inside him. There was something appealing about Faolan. He was dangerous, fun, and sexy all at once. Faolan was a man who'd be ballsy enough to push past his barriers, forcing him to take things to the next level.

He could do that.

"You talk too much, Faolan."

Lowering his body so their chests pressed fully against each other, he moved his mouth to Faolan's ear and sucked hard. Groaning, Faolan clamped his hand to the back of Gar's head, holding him in place.

"Fuck. Say my name again."

"Faolan."

Faolan bucked his hips, grinding his hard cock against Gar's. "If you don't fuck me soon, I'm going to tear your ship apart."

Gar nipped at his neck, running his tongue over the sensitive skin as he reached down between them and began to fumble with Faolan's belt.

"Now you're the one wearing too much clothing," he said into Faolan's shoulder.

Within a moment the belt was free. Hands competed as both men pushed open the soft leather pants and yanked them over Faolan's hips. Gar had to stop long enough to pull both the pants and Faolan's boots off. Another quick action had Faolan stripped of his shirt, leaving him naked under Gar. Gar let his gaze wander over the expanse of flesh before him.

"Beautiful," he whispered.

Before Faolan had a chance to retort with a smart-ass response, Gar wrapped a hand around his cock and squeezed hard. The groan that escaped Faolan was low and vibrated in his chest. Faolan tugged him down for another searing kiss.

"Fuck me, hunter." He ground his cock against Gar's thigh. "We both need this."

"Only because of the drug."

"If that's what you need to tell yourself."

It was. This was sex, pure and simple—because the last person he could become attached to was a pompous ass like Faolan. No, he'd use the pirate how he wanted, take what he needed to regain control, and then get back to the matter at hand.

For once, he'd enjoy himself and leave worrying about the future to another day.

Dipping his head down, he captured Faolan's nipple in his mouth to suck the peak hard. He ran his tongue over the sensitive tip until Faolan groaned loud enough to fill the room. Gar's cock pressed painfully against the fabric of his pants, desperate to get out. No, he would put off his pleasure until the last possible moment if he wanted to make this memorable for both of them. He needed a distraction.

Shifting his body, he nipped and licked his way down Faolan's body until he reached the other man's impressive cock. He felt the pirate stifle a moan as his mouth hovered a few inches from the swollen, purple tip.

"Do you want me to suck you?" Gar's voice sounded hoarse even to his own ears.

Faolan sighed. "Fuck yes."

Without any further encouragement, Gar swiped his tongue across the broad head of Faolan's shaft. Faolan's hands pulled at his hair to move him closer.

"My ship, my rules." He knew it would frustrate Faolan.

"You're a cock tease, hunter."

"Don't play with fire unless you're willing to get burned."

Before Faolan could retort, Gar sucked his cock hard, taking most of it into his mouth and down his throat. The captain's loud moan was reward enough, but added to the sweet taste of skin and pre-cum in his mouth, it was enough to drive Gar over the edge. Unable to stop himself, he reached down to stroke himself through his pants as he devoured Faolan, taking as much as he could. The velvet smoothness of Faolan's balls and shaft was unlike anything he'd experienced before. This was different from the sex he'd had in the past—whether from the drug or simply due to the overwhelming presence of the captain, he felt himself falling toward total abandon. He ran his tongue across every inch of skin he could find, memorizing the scent and taste, ignoring the stir of feelings deep inside his chest.

"Dear fucking gods," Faolan hissed. He tugged on Gar's head as his cock twitched against Gar's tongue. "I'm going to come."

The pirate's voice was heavy with desire, bordering on desperate. He knew they both needed this release in order for things to return to some semblance of normalcy. With a smile, he pulled off Faolan's cock with a pop, and squeezed the base of the shaft to prevent his release. Faolan groaned loudly and thumped his head back against the sofa cushion.

Gar placed a kiss against Faolan's flat stomach. "Coming is a bad thing. Bad, bad."

"No, no, it really isn't. Teasing is."

"Who's teasing?"

"You are."

"So sucking your cock is teasing?"

"When you stop seconds before I blow in your mouth and *still* refuse to fuck me? Yes."

Gar again squeezed Faolan's cock as hard as he could, dragging a groan from him. Rising to his knees, he slowly undid his pants, enjoying the way Faolan's eyes hungrily encouraged him on.

"Take it off for me, hunter."

"You don't deserve it, pirate."

"Then make me earn it."

The cool air kissed the top of his cock as it finally sprang free from his pants. Before Gar could stop him, Faolan pushed the material down over his hips, exposing him completely. What he hadn't expected was for Faolan's hand to curl around the base of his cock, the pressure a sweet promise of his impending release.

Looking into Faolan's eyes, Gar was surprised by the depth of desire he saw reflected there. The captain could fuck any man, woman, or alien he wanted. But at that moment, every ounce of his passion was directed toward Gar—the effect was damn near blinding. He felt like the only man in the universe who could give Faolan what he wanted.

Biting his bottom lip, he gazed into his new lover's face. His control threatened to break again. He stiffened, leaning over Faolan to look him in the eye.

"Suck me."

The captain's groan told Gar he had him where he wanted him. Gar shifted forward but still forced the pirate to slide across the couch in order to wrap his lips around Gar's swollen shaft.

Pure heaven. The heat from Faolan's mouth enveloped his cock as Faolan played with his balls. The contact sent tendrils of pleasure coursing through his body, setting his skin on fire, making it sensitive to the air and heat around him. When Faolan ran his tongue from the base of Gar's sac to the tip of his cock, he couldn't help but moan and drive his fingers into Faolan's soft brown hair.

"Your mouth is wicked." He breathed the words.

Faolan smiled around his shaft. Thankfully, the man knew when to stop talking. When Faolan's tongue circled the head of Gar's cock repeatedly, Gar broke out into a sweat. His breath came in short pants until he was sure he was going to pass out from lack of oxygen.

Finally pulling Faolan's face away, he looked down into those beautiful blue eyes. Without thinking, he leaned forward and kissed the man hard, driving his tongue into Faolan's mouth, needing to feel something—any sort of connection. Gods, he was so tired of being alone.

"I'm going to fuck you now, pirate."

Surprisingly, Faolan's eyes dipped closed for a second before his smug, sexy look returned. "Bet I last longer than you."

Gar pushed him back hard against the couch. "That's a bet I'll take."

Pausing only long enough to strip away his remaining clothing, Gar pressed every inch of his body against Faolan's. Reveling in the feel of bare flesh on flesh, needing to absorb the other man's strength and heat. Their cocks, hot and hard, rubbed against each other, the pressure almost too much to take. But he wasn't going to lose.

Reaching between them, he slid his hand over Faolan's cock, then down to press against the tight ring of his ass. Faolan gasped as Gar's finger penetrated, but he didn't look away. Instead, he ran his hand up Gar's arm, over his shoulder and neck, threading his fingers through Gar's hair. The touch was almost loving as Faolan caressed his skin. Fuck, he was reading too much into a simple embrace. Closing his eyes, he increased the pressure on Faolan's ass, knowing he'd need to prepare him for what he was about to do.

"Right pocket of my pants," Faolan moaned.

It only took a second to retrieve the small bottle of lubricant. Raising a single eyebrow at him, Gar waited. Faolan chuckled.

"You caught me in the arms of two lovers. What did you expect?" He had a point.

Squeezing a generous amount of the gel into his palm, Gar gripped his own cock, running a hand up and down the length, never once tearing his gaze away from Faolan. Despite the pirate's reputation of being a voracious lover, the look he gave Gar was nothing short of admiring.

Gar pressed a lubed finger into Faolan's ass, enjoying the pleasure clouding his eyes. When Gar added a second, then third finger, Faolan's hips bucked, and he grabbed at the edges of the couch as if to hold on for dear life.

"It's been so long—" Faolan started before biting on his lower lip, stopping the words.

"You won't have to wait much longer."

With that, Gar removed his fingers and pushed Faolan's legs wide, positioning himself against the tight opening. The pressure against the tip of his cock forced his eyes closed so he could enjoy the sensation. Steadily, he moved forward. Only once he was buried balls-deep, and Faolan's body couldn't take any more, did he pause to catch his breath. "So good."

"I promise, it will be much better if you start to *move*." Faolan encouraged him with a soft bucking of his hips.

"Impatient. I'll take care of you."

"You better, hunter."

Gar wrapped his hand around Faolan's cock and squeezed hard. "I never go back on a promise."

Words were lost between them then. Gar began to gently move his hips, driving himself in and out of Faolan's ass with slow precision, angling to graze Faolan's prostate. He somehow managed to keep perfect time with his hand as he stroked Faolan's shaft, squeezing at the base, knowing the pressure would drive Faolan close to the edge without pushing him over.

The sound of their moans, gasps, and sweat-covered bodies slapping against each other filled the cabin. Gar couldn't think, could only feel. Gods, this was what it was like to abandon himself . . . He *never* did this. Heat and the smell of sex were so strong, but so was the silent promise of something else. Something he had no intention of dwelling on. People like him didn't deserve those types of considerations.

Faolan's fingers dug into his hips, pulling him forward. Gar let his body weight drop forward while keeping his hand pistoning over Faolan's cock. Their chests were close, but he managed to keep them from pressing together. He knew he would be lost soon if he didn't do something quickly. A shift of his hips caused the angle to change, ensuring that he was hitting the one spot guaranteed to drive Faolan crazy.

He felt Faolan's cock swell and pulse in his hand before the pirate's body stiffened. Faolan cried out as cum shot from his shaft, his body shaking violently with the release. Gar milked every ounce of cum from him before he released his cock, then Gar fell forward, clinging to him tightly. The heat of Faolan's chest penetrated, increasing tenfold when his arms wrapped around him, pulling him closer.

"Come for me," Faolan whispered. "Please."

That single word was all it took to push Gar over the edge. His balls tightened, and he let out a raw cry, pounding as hard as he could into Faolan. The rush of pleasure seemed to last forever as he trembled and his cock pulsed.

Things blurred for several minutes. The first sounds he heard upon regaining full consciousness were Faolan's soft murmurs in his ear.

"So amazing, Gar. I've never been taken like that before."

Unable to form a coherent thought, let alone speak, he simply buried his face against Faolan's neck, placing a single chaste kiss in the crook of the other man's shoulder. Faolan's skin was warm, tasted of salt and musk. He inhaled the scent, and for the briefest of moments, he relaxed. Strong arms adjusted around his back, a hand coming to rest lazily against the nape of his neck, teasing the short hair.

"Aren't you full of surprises, hunter."

That was all it took to shatter his fragile sense of peace. Everything came rushing back—why they were here, what his objective was. Losing himself deep inside a perfect body—the perfect fuck—wasn't something he could afford to do.

With more regret than he'd ever admit, he pushed himself onto his forearms to look into Faolan's face, searching his eyes for any sign that this was anything more than a quick lay. While he saw many things, he didn't find the answer he wanted.

"This changes nothing."

Shock, tinged with something remotely akin to hurt, flashed across Faolan's face for the briefest of seconds, but then the cocky grin was firmly back in place. "That's where you're wrong, pretty boy. It changes everything."

Gar slipped his soft cock from Faolan's ass and stood, naked. He let his gaze linger on Faolan for a moment before he bent down and picked up his now-wrinkled suit. For some odd reason, he couldn't make eye contact any more.

"You can sleep here. I'll be in the cockpit once I change."

He started to leave when he heard Faolan chuckle. He responded, knowing he wasn't keeping the annoyance from his voice. "What?"

"The code for the disk is alpha-4502-wolf. Take me to my ship, hunter."

"I thought you said it was voice locked?"

"It is. But if you use that code, anyone can access the information inside. Always need to have a backup just in case."

A sudden flash of irritation ripped through him, but he knew that was what Faolan had wanted. Memorizing the code and ignoring the arrogant captain, he triggered the bio sensor on his door.

Before leaving, he looked over his shoulder at Faolan. "I believe I won the bet. You better be ready to pay up, pirate."

CHAPTER
FOUR

B *astard bounty hunter.* Cocky, self-righteous jerk who thought he was better than everyone else around him.

At least he was good in bed. Or on the couch, as it were.

Faolan had recovered enough from his orgasm and the remnants of the erotigen to get up, wipe the cum from his stomach with his shirt, and get dressed. Left with only his coat and pants to wear—which admittedly was a good look on him—he relaxed to roll the events of the past few hours around in his head.

Ten minutes after Gar had disappeared behind the locked second door, he reemerged wearing another pristine suit. The boy had issues for sure.

"Got somewhere I can clean up?"

Gar's gaze lingered over his body just long enough to reveal continued interest. "I'll let you use my shower once we put the coordinates to your ship in my navigation computer."

"That sounds promising." The teasing came naturally to Faolan, an easy mechanism for keeping people from asking too many questions. No one took him seriously until it was too late. "Maybe I'll get to be the one doing the fucking next time."

Gar stiffened, jerked the hem of his waistcoat down, and strode past where Faolan stood. "Need to get us moving."

Faolan chuckled. The boy wasn't a natural bottom. It was something he would have to work on if they were going to continue to play.

Running his hands through his hair, he sauntered behind Gar into the ship's cockpit, admiring the quick flash of Gar's trousered ass before it slid into the pilot's seat. It was completely unfair Faolan wouldn't have a chance at sinking his cock into it—at least not for a while. No, that wouldn't do at all. It had been a long time since he'd had to work at getting someone into bed, but for once he didn't mind the challenge. Something about Gar resonated with him, eliciting curiosity he hadn't experienced in an extremely long time.

Gar's hands slid over the control panel, his long fingers dancing easily over the controls. He maneuvered the ship into position for the dimension gate. Faolan leaned over the back of the chair, pressing his nose against Gar's hair. He still smelled like sex.

"Stop that." Gar stiffened, pulling away slightly.

"Why?"

"I don't like it."

"Is it a rule that I'm not allowed to be close to the man who just fucked me senseless? Because if it is, then I think you need to get a new rule book."

Gar turned his face enough that Faolan's nose brushed against his temple. Heat rose from the hunter, and a pleasant tingle wormed its way down Faolan's neck. Gods, there had to be drugs still in his system for him to be reacting this strongly. He'd have to check with the dealer later to find out if any other surprises had been included in that concoction.

"I . . . No, it's not a rule. I just don't like people hanging over my shoulder."

Faolan didn't miss the defensive tone in Gar's voice. There was something more to it though—an uncertainty undercutting the previously cocksure bounty hunter.

Interesting.

Not wanting to back down, he rubbed his nose against the fine hairs of Gar's sideburns. The scent of soap mixed with sweat invaded his senses, making his cock twitch.

"Again I ask you why? You know I'm not going to hurt you, and we've already proved that we are *fantastic* together."

"Are you always this much of a bastard, Captain?"

Faolan chuckled and kissed Gar's cheek before he backed off and fell into the copilot's chair. "I'm actually behaving. I wouldn't want you to turn nasty and kick me out the airlock or something."

Gar stared at him with such intensity, Faolan's stomach flipped and his heartbeat kicked up several notches. He refused to look away though, knowing Gar would take it as a sign of weakness. Instead he lifted his foot and pressed it against the edge of the computer console in front of him, locking his fingers behind his head.

"You gonna put in the coordinates so we can get going?"

Gar rolled his eyes before returning his attention to the navigation control. "We're still a few minutes out from the gate. I've input the code you gave me, and it's feeding the rendezvous point into the nav system now."

"So, that means we have time to talk?"

"I have nothing to say to you, Wolf." The retort was a quick and practiced reflex.

Faolan pressed his hand to his heart. "You wound me. I'm good enough for you to shove your cock up my ass, but not good enough to converse with? Really, most people would say you have your priorities backward . . . but I'm never one to turn down great sex."

He'd meant the snap response to be teasing, but Gar squirmed in his chair, a light blush creeping across his pale cheeks. "Sorry."

Whoa. "For what, hunter? I'm just harassing you. Bit of fun."

The computer chose that moment to pop to life, warning sensors echoing loudly in the small quarters. The static beacon markers floated in a straight line in space, leading directly to the dimension gate. They started to shift, adjusting to the *Geilt*'s size and shape the closer they got.

Gar's body relaxed as he began to move the ship into position. "We're approaching the dimension gate now. You might want to strap in to be safe."

"Not confident in your ability to get me through in one piece?" But Faolan sat up and slipped the restraint across his chest.

"Been a while since you've been on a personal cruiser, hasn't it?"

"Well, there was that one time a few years ago with the Damarian freighter captain. She had legs that went on for light-years and the biggest set of—"

The jerk of the ship flying into the dimension gate sent Faolan's head snapping back. The crack of his skull connecting with the hard seat echoed in his ears as the world around him spun. Outside, space folded in on itself as the fabric of the universe split open, allowing the ship to slide effortlessly through. The effects of the dimension jump were increased in the small ship—the thinning of the air, the slight electrical charge filling the cabin, the way his skin felt hot and cold at the same time. The whole thing left him breathless and dizzy by the time they had passed through to the other side. It was the only reason he didn't immediately notice Gar's hysterical laughter.

"The look on your face," Gar managed to get out in between peals.

Faolan really liked the sound. Putting on an exaggerated frown, he twisted in his chair and rubbed the back of his head. "Do you always laugh at the misfortune of others? If that's so, I might have to reconsider our working arrangement."

Gar's laugh petered into a soft chuckle, punctuated by side looks at Faolan. "No, not normally."

There it was! A crack in the ice encasing the bounty hunter, and Faolan had caused it. It shouldn't have pleased him so much, but the soft smile Gar gave him did something odd to his insides.

The computer beeped again, capturing Gar's attention. "We're clear of the gate and your disk is feeding the next set of coordinates. How many more jumps?"

"Three."

Gar nodded. "It will take some time. The *Geilt* is fast, but the engines need to reset."

The idea of being alone with Gar for the next few days suddenly didn't seem so painful. "So how long do we have to wait until we can make it to the next gate?"

"Ten hours."

Not nearly enough time for what Faolan wanted to do—peel away Gar's layers and examine what was beneath. He had a feeling no one had managed to get far below the surface of this guy in a long time. Perhaps Krieg, but Faolan doubted he wanted to screw Gar. Maybe he did—who knew anymore. Faolan had a feeling he could spend months with Gar and still not know much about him. He'd have to make the most of the next few days—it would do for a start.

Running a finger down the length of his throat, he gave Gar his most seductive grin. "Whatever shall we do to pass the time?"

He kept his gaze fixed on Gar, knowing the other man wouldn't miss the invitation. Part of Faolan hoped he'd take him up on it right away. With the erotigen still lingering in his system, the sex would be *amazing*. Surprisingly though, another part of him hoped Gar would say no. The chase was proving just as entertaining as the catch—a rare occurrence in his considerable experience. He actually wanted to find out more about a lover.

Shit, this was the first time in years he'd actually wanted to be with someone more than once. And wasn't *that* an interesting twist of events.

Gar seemed to be fighting his own internal battle, if the frown on his face was anything to go by. It made him look much younger than he had earlier. Faolan had never seen such rigid adherence to rules, combined with such deadly determination and precision. It was off, wrong, and Faolan couldn't imagine what had happened to make Gar that way.

"How old are you?" he asked as he slipped the seat's restraint from his body.

Gar's eyes snapped open wide, and he twisted to face him. "What?"

Faolan chuckled. "You'd think I'd just asked you to fuck your grandmother. How *old* are you? It shouldn't be that challenging a question."

Gar opened and closed his mouth several times before shaking his head. "Why do you want to know?"

Faolan rolled his eyes. "Thought it might be nice to get to know you a bit, hunter. But if it's that big a deal, forget I asked. I'll take advantage of the time to have a shower."

He didn't wait to see if he had Gar's permission to use the facilities. He knew they were located on the other side of the secured door. It didn't even matter that he didn't have the security code to gain access—a locked door had never stopped him in the past. Getting to his feet, he left the cockpit, smiling when the door didn't slide shut as he left.

"Where do you think you're going?"

Faolan didn't have to turn around to know there was a scowl on Gar's face. "Shower. Remember, you promised I could use it once we jumped?"

"Yes, but you can't go wandering around unattended—"

Faolan spun on his heel. "Right, your bloody fucking rules. Do you honestly expect me to sit here on this ship for three days and stay in this room? No shower, no clothing, no food?"

Gar's teeth were clenched so hard, Faolan could hear the grinding from across the room. "I expect you to respect my home."

"How many times do I have to say it? Respect is—"

"Earned, I know. I've been a gracious host."

"Hello, knife to my throat?"

"You were snooping in my things."

"Gods, you're bitchy."

"Fuck you, pirate."

"You've already done that, hunter. Not sure if I want a repeat performance if this is how you are afterward."

Faolan crossed his arms and leaned against the wall beside the door that led to the private quarters of the ship. They weren't at an impasse so much as he refused to give Gar a way out. In many ways, Gar reminded him of how he'd been after escaping his home planet years ago—scared to death to let anyone get too close. Keeping people at arm's length hadn't helped though. The sooner Gar realized that, the sooner he'd be able to lead a somewhat normal life. As normal as possible for a bounty hunter who roamed the far reaches of this galactic sector, at any rate.

Gar's hands were balled tight by his sides. Faolan knew he'd put the concealed blades back on, but wasn't sure if he was now debating using them or if the twitch of his wrists was an unconscious habit when he felt threatened.

Faolan thrust a hip out to the side, the dried cum on his skin stretching and cracking, causing him to frown.

"Look, I'm sorry I've thrown such a glitch into your perfectly working system. If you want to contact Krieg and have someone else deal with this, that's fine by me. But if you're going to see this through, I'd like to have a shower. Maybe steal a clean shirt from you. I'll let you watch me the whole time, if it makes you feel any better. No tricks, no games."

"Asshole." Gar marched across the room and pressed a code into the panel. "If you touch anything—"

"I'll cut my own balls off and hand them to you. You won't have to worry about a thing."

He rolled away from the wall and went to move past Gar when a hand on his shoulder stopped him. Looking up fast, he was surprised by the openness he saw in Gar's eyes.

"I'm twenty-four."

Gods almighty. "You're just a kid."

"Hardly." Gar motioned with his chin. "Shower is through there, Captain."

Faolan found it hard to reconcile Gar's reputation with the man standing before him. At twenty-four, Faolan himself had barely gotten a position on a ship, let alone earned a reputation like Gar Stitt's.

"Captain?" Gar frowned, his hand slipping from Faolan's shoulder.

He mentally shook himself and forced a grin. "Better have enough hot water on this bucket. I hate it when it runs cold halfway through. I plan on taking my time. Been ages since I've had a good long shower."

Gar rolled his eyes, but otherwise didn't respond. Instead of puzzling over the man himself, Faolan concentrated on uncovering the secrets of his ship. He followed Gar down a short, wide corridor lined with four doors. One had a red light above it, indicating the passageway to systems and engineering. Gar led him to the last one on the left. Instead of a code, he pressed his thumb to a panel.

"DNA scanner?" Faolan crowded him to look over his shoulder.

"Thinking of cutting off my thumb?"

"I would rather die than damage those talented digits."

That earned him another chuckle. Faolan rested his chin on Gar's shoulder, mirroring their earlier position. "You should do that more often."

"What?"

"Laugh. It sounds . . . nice."

Gar turned and cocked an eyebrow. "*Nice?*"

"I'd say sexy, but I'm fearful of my life."

Gar's lips twitched, but he managed to hold back the smile. "I'll accept 'sexy' over '*nice*.' I'm not a *nice* man."

Neither of them moved for a moment. Faolan wanted nothing more than to wrap his arms around Gar and hold on.

Fuck, what the hell is wrong with me?

Straightening, he pulled back, not wanting Gar to notice his reawakening erection. "Where's the shower again?"

Gar cleared his throat. "Yeah. Right through here."

Gar moved stiffly through the room. It took Faolan's brain a few seconds to realize they were in Gar's bedroom. By the time he was ready to take advantage of the location, they'd already walked through to the bathroom.

"Shower is there. It's recycled water heated by the ship's engines, so you won't have to worry about it getting cold. It's also purified so you won't have to worry about catching anything. I'll get you a clean shirt and bring it in."

"Not going to watch?" Faolan winked at Gar, slipping the jacket from his shoulders. "I can be quite entertaining when I need to be."

Again, he preened as Gar stared at his naked chest. He popped open the fly of his pants, giving his hips a shake until the fabric slid down over his hips.

Gar looked away, bracing his hand against the doorframe. The reach was high enough, his suit jacket pulled tight across his biceps. "I'll get that shirt."

Before Faolan had a chance to tease him further, Gar left the room.

CHAPTER

FIVE

Gar's head ached. His balls ached too, which was surprising considering how hard he'd come only a short time ago. With his back to the shower room, he made his way over to the storage wall and pressed the button to release the clothing drawer. He rummaged through until he found a clean undershirt. It wasn't new, but he didn't think Faolan would be comfortable in one of his dress shirts. The image of Faolan wearing one of the crisp shirts sent an involuntary shiver through him. Closing his eyes, he sucked in a deep breath and tried to calm the chaos in his head.

Faolan had only been on his ship for a few hours, and Gar felt like his life was splitting apart. No one pushed him like the pirate—no one had ever looked beyond the suits and the blades enough to know how. Even Jason, with all of his lessons over the years, hadn't bothered to get too close. Gar was a tool, a means for Jason to accomplish whatever ends he determined relevant. While Jason certainly had been there for him, offering a certain measure of support and guidance since his father's death, there was still a barrier between them. Not that it mattered to Gar—he liked the solitude.

His fingers bunched tight around the cloth, and he shoved the drawer shut, marching back toward the shower. For the sake of his sanity, he really needed to get Faolan off his ship before he did something he'd regret. The sound of water echoed in the small room. Gar slowed his approach as he heard Faolan let out a low moan. *What the hell?*

"You alive in there?" Gar tossed the shirt over his shoulder and peeked around the corner.

Faolan stood naked under the spray, head bent forward. Water ran in rivulets down his back. "Gods, this feels amazing. I always miss my shower when I'm not home on my ship."

Gar couldn't help but follow the water's path as it flowed down between the cheeks of Faolan's ass, over the smooth skin of his thighs on its way down to the drain in the floor. The stark white of the shower stall made the captain's tanned skin look even darker. The tattoo on his arm seemed to glisten, making the dragon come alive as Faolan stretched and twisted his body. Faolan chose that moment to look up, deep-blue gaze peering out at Gar from between the wet strands of his long brown hair.

"Want to join me?"

There it was again, the note of amusement and lust that the pirate hit so perfectly. This time, Gar couldn't blame his reaction on the erotigen. He wanted to jerk his suit free from his body and press himself hard against Faolan's back so he could feel how good the water was on his skin. The distance Gar usually kept from the people around him didn't seem to apply to Faolan. The pirate managed to walk right up to his barriers and push against them. Instead of his normal impulse to run and hide, Gar found he didn't mind. Shaking those thoughts from his head, he ignored the pang of loneliness in his gut.

No, don't do this. Don't get too close or you know what will happen.

Faolan wasn't easily deterred. With one hand braced against the shower wall, he captured some soap from the dispenser on the wall and pressed the foamy substance to his hairless chest. Small bubbles formed across his pecs, catching on his nipples and the natural divots of his skin. Gar's chest tightened. He forced himself to breathe in slow, even breaths.

"The hot water is nice. Good to know you splurged on the system when you got your ship." Faolan smiled as his hand circled the soap slowly down his chest to his stomach.

Gar swallowed hard. "Need to have some perks."

Faolan cocked his head to the side as his eyes slid half-closed. "Oh, I love it when your accent gets deep like that. Makes me think you're enjoying the show."

"What show is that? I don't see any entertainment." He was surprised at how easy it was to slip into the sexual banter. He liked it—which scared him as much as it turned him on.

Faolan's answering smirk should have warned him, but he was still surprised by the man's next words. "Well, I do believe I lost a bet to you earlier. Maybe a little entertainment is payment enough? What do you think?"

Gar forced his eyes to remain locked with Faolan's and not dip down to watch the trail his fingers were making in the soap bubbles around his belly button. "Guess it depends on how good you can make the show."

"I can make it *very* good. Won awards for it, in fact."

"I find that hard to believe."

Faolan's hand stopped barely an inch from where his erect cock now stood hard against his stomach. "How about another bet? I'll put on a show good enough to make you come in your pants. If I do, I get to do whatever I want to you later on."

Warning screams ripped through his head as his brain tried to win out over his lust-addled body. "It will never happen."

"So sure about that? Maybe you really are made of ice." Faolan licked his lips. "I'm willing to take the risk and find out."

Gar knew this was a bad idea. Why, after all the years of careful planning, was Faolan able to blast through his control like this? He'd been alone for years and it had been enough for him. Reaching out to the occasional stranger when he needed a fuck to keep him sane. Why then was Faolan so different? Why did Gar want to sink into his embrace and forget the universe and all the shit it had piled on his shoulders?

Still, he'd never met anyone who could push his buttons the way Faolan could, turn him on the way the pirate had in their short acquaintance. It could be fun . . . which was something people frequently told him he should have. And he had never been able to back down from a challenge.

He cocked an eyebrow. "And what if I win?"

Faolan made a show of considering. "What could I possibly offer a man who appears to want nothing? I guess it's only fair that you get the same. If I can't do as promised, then I'm yours to do what you want with."

"Anything?" Scenarios rolled through his head at an alarming rate.

"I'm a man of my word. You should know that by now, Stitt. Anything you want me to do, I'm yours—*if* you win."

"You're on." *Bad idea, Gar. This will end poorly.* He was already regretting the mad impulse that had driven him to this contest of wills.

Faolan grinned, adjusting himself by leaning his forearm against the shower stall. Gar took an involuntary step backward until the firm plane of the wall pressed against his shoulder blades.

"Take your jacket off," Faolan said, his voice a low rumble. "The vest too. Off."

Without thinking, Gar started working the buttons. The air was heavy with steam, causing a trickle of sweat to bead on the back of his neck and roll beneath his collar. Faolan watched, an intense look on his face. Realizing his actions were having an impact on Faolan, Gar slowed his pace, taking his time to slide his fingertip into the holes to pull each button free.

"Gods, those hands of yours . . . should be illegal."

"What makes you think they're not?" Gar freed the last button and slipped the jacket and vest from his arms. Turning toward the bedroom, he tossed the garments on the berth. "There, satisfied?"

Faolan nodded. "Very. Now I can see the wet spot your cum will make when you blow your load."

Gar gasped at the lewd image. Stumbling, he adjusted his stance, widening his legs to adjust for his growing erection. "Bastard."

"You agreed to the bet. I'm just doing my part to make the best temptation possible." Faolan reached over and grabbed another handful of soap from the dispenser. "I'll want to make sure I'm nice and clean. Never know when I'll have to impress someone."

This time Faolan didn't stop his downward progress to his cock. Gar watched, slightly awed, as Faolan reached around the bottom of his balls and tugged them gently. He rubbed a small circular pattern across the tightening sac with his thumb, humming pleasantly as he did.

"This would be so much better if it was your hand, Stitt. Those long fingers of yours felt so good wrapped around my cock. You really know how to work a man."

Gar fought to keep his eyes open and his body still. He couldn't react or he'd lose control. He never lost control.

"You're a man of detail, something I really appreciate. Though I get the impression you don't spent a lot of time with your lovers once you're done fucking them. Still, the ones you've had must have commented on your skill. Eh? How you learned as much as you could about them before running away?"

Faolan's fingers dipped behind his sac now. The angle was all wrong for him to actually reach his hole, but he must have been close. Gar's cock was now painfully hard, but he wouldn't touch it. No, he was stronger than a few suggestive words and the sight of an attractive naked man in his shower.

"Yup, you'd make it your mission to find out all the spots I like to be touched, wouldn't you?" Faolan shifted his body once more, spreading his legs wide. "For example, I don't think it would take you any time to find out that I like to have my cock stroked slowly but firmly. Like this."

Fascinated, Gar watched Faolan palm his balls briefly before wrapping his hand around the base of his cock. He squeezed hard enough that Gar could see the tip darkening. Faolan let out another low moan, only this time he punctuated it with a gasp as he stroked up the length of his shaft. Faolan's eyes rolled back into his head before he squeezed them shut and his body shuddered.

"It's so fucking hot having you watch me do this, Gar."

Gar's hand was pressed to his groin before the sigh left his mouth. The way Faolan said his name nearly pushed him over the edge. *Gods damn it, how did he get me so close?*

"Make sure you're watching, Gar. I want you to learn all my secrets so the next time I'm spread out beneath you, you'll know how to make me scream."

Faolan didn't hesitate, didn't slow down. With sure, even strokes, he worked his fist over his shaft. Without Gar realizing, his breathing increased in rhythm until it came in time with each stroke. Steam from the water billowed around him, making his shirt cling in damp patches.

Faolan grinned, keeping his eyes squeezed shut. "I can hear you over there. You like what you see?" When Gar didn't respond immediately, Faolan slowed down his stroking. "Tell me you like this. Tell me what it's doing to you."

"I . . ." Gar forced his hand away from his cock and pressed it flat against the wall. "Yes, I like this. I like watching you stroke yourself."

"Tell me what you want me to do. What you'd be doing to me if I were to let you touch me."

So many things came to mind. "I'd . . . tug on your balls just hard enough to make you moan."

Faolan didn't hesitate. Releasing his cock, he moved lower again until his sac was fixed in the middle of his hand before pulling. Throwing his head back, he opened his eyes, catching Gar's gaze before letting out a groan. "Don't leave me hanging."

Fuck, fuck, damn it. "Your ass. Use the soap and shove a finger in there. Open yourself up for me."

Gar would have laughed at the way Faolan's hand shook as he grabbed for the soap—would have laughed if he wasn't so close to the edge, aching and wanting to fuck. Faolan never once broke eye contact as he reached behind himself and pressed a finger into his ass.

"I'm still loose from when you took me earlier. I bet I still have your cum inside me."

"Another," Gar swallowed, gasping for air. "Another finger. Two inside you. Do it."

"Yes," Faolan hissed. "Not as good as you. Not as big as your cock."

"Three, then. You can take it."

"Want you. Please."

"No. You promised me a show. That's what I want. Now three fingers."

Faolan's lips fell open as he panted, letting water roll down his face and into his mouth. "You must be so hard right now. Remembering how tight I was around your cock. I haven't let anyone fuck me in a long time. Did you know that? You were my first in years. You felt so big when you pushed your way inside. Ah!"

Gar's body burned as Faolan writhed under his own touch. He needed to touch himself, shove his hand down the front of his trousers and jerk himself off. Shaking his head, he did his best to fight past the blast of lust. He had to win.

Words spilled from their mouths, each trying to talk over and outdo the other with their attempts. Gar's body vibrated with the need to release, his fragile restraint quickly waning.

"Curl your fingers, Faolan. Spread yourself nice and wide for me, so I could fuck you if I wanted."

"I don't want to be too loose. Need to feel every inch of you. I love how big and thick you are."

"Oh, you'll feel it. Just like you'll feel it when I jerk you off in time with my thrusts."

"I'll squeeze my ass so hard around your shaft, you'll beg me to let you come. Only if you're good."

"I'll fuck you so hard against that wall, they'll hear you scream back on Tybal. Then you'll be the one begging for more."

Faolan cried out, pulling his fingers quickly from his ass only to wrap them around his cock. He pushed away from the wall only to mirror Gar's position, back flush with the shower stall and stance wide. The only difference was he wasn't attempting to halt his orgasm, and Gar was.

"Gods, I wish you could see yourself, Gar. Panting, and your skin is so flushed. That cock of yours looks like it's going to burst through the front of your pants. I bet you'd like nothing more than for me to drop to my knees in front of you and swallow you whole. Maybe I'd tease your asshole. I bet you'd like that a lot. I'd take such good care of you, make you see stars and catch you when you fell. Come on, Gar. Let me hear you. I want you to come for me. Please. Come now. Please, please, *please*."

He couldn't stop it. Didn't want to. The second he pressed down on his erection, Gar closed his eyes and came. The scream that escaped sounded nothing like him. Pulse after pulse of cum shot from him, warm and wet in his already damp clothing.

Only after the rush of pleasure subsided did his legs give out, and he slumped to the floor. It took a minute for him to realize Faolan was still watching, still stroking himself. "Oh shit. So gorgeous when you've come unraveled like that. Just for me."

Faolan's cock erupted, his cum caught by the rush of water from the shower to be washed away. He found enough strength to press the Off button, ending the hiss of the water, before he slid to the floor himself. The relative quiet that filled the room was far from unpleasant or awkward.

The man on the other side of the room, a man who by all rights should be locked away in the bowels of his ship, had now caught Gar off guard twice. Each time, instead of the crashing disappointment that normally followed such encounters for him, Gar was overcome with an uneasy sense of peace. Maybe Gar had finally found someone who could understand him.

"I won," Faolan said softly. "Barely."

Gar opened his mouth to protest, argue, defend himself, when Faolan held up his hand. "Don't. Whatever you were about to say, just . . . don't. I've had two amazing orgasms in the past hour and a half. My brain is officially past due."

Gar nodded. "Truce, then."

"Until my brain comes back to life? Yes." Faolan struggled, but managed to push himself to his knees, only to crawl over to Gar. "You're all messy again."

"I've ruined this suit."

Faolan pressed a chaste kiss to Gar's cheek. "I like you messy."

"How much longer will you be on my ship?" Gar scowled, but there was none of his regular venom behind it. He couldn't be bothered to muster it up. It didn't feel right in any regard.

"Let me clean you up." Faolan's breath somehow managed to be warm against Gar's already hot skin.

He didn't protest as Faolan made short work of the buttons of his shirt and the one that held his trousers closed. Faolan let out a low whistle when he dipped his hand into the small opening the angle afforded and swirled a finger through the cum in Gar's pants.

"Yup, I definitely like you messy."

Clothing was stripped then, with the occasional press of skin against skin. Gar tried not to notice the way Faolan moved or how he remained in constant contact with Gar's body as they washed away his cum and sweat.

Faolan swayed into Gar as they finally left the bathroom. "Bed. I need to close my eyes for a bit."

"What makes you think you've earned it?"

Gar was only teasing, but Faolan stopped short. Gar turned to face him, only to be surprised by the open sincerity in his expression. "Gar, just for a bit. I'm . . . I need to rest."

There was something wrong. It wasn't right for a man of Faolan's strength to look utterly exhausted so suddenly. Nodding, Gar's concern won over as he shifted to wrap an arm around Faolan's waist. "I changed the sheets this morning."

"I would never doubt they were clean. Bit of an obsession with you, isn't it? Being clean?"

"Shut up and lie down."

They crawled onto the bed, one after the other, their bodies close but not touching.

"Listen, Gar—"

"Stop. Just . . . sleep. We have time to talk later."

Gar watched Faolan nod and close his eyes. Within minutes, the captain's breathing evened out and it was clear he was sleeping. Shifting only when he knew he wouldn't wake the other man, Gar let out a shuddering breath. This was such a bad idea.

What the hell am I getting myself into?

CHAPTER

SIX

Faolan woke up feeling surprisingly well rested. That in itself was odd considering what he'd put his body through over the past few months. It was rare for him to be able to sleep through the night, even more so in a bed clearly not his. Rolling onto his side, he buried his nose into the soft fullness of the pillow and breathed in deep.

Gar.

His scent clung to the fabric, cocooning Faolan in warmth. He didn't remember what had happened after falling into bed. A quick glance beneath the covers revealed his still-naked body, though any water had long since been absorbed into the bedding.

Where the hell was Gar?

He lay still long enough to enjoy the warmth for a few more minutes before throwing the covers back with a groan and sliding none too gracefully from the bed. A big bed with room for two, no simple ship's berth tucked against a wall. He really needed to get one of those onto the *Belle Kurve*. Mace would kick his ass for making such an indulgent purchase, though, especially since she would never be able to take advantage of it. He preferred to avoid pissing off his first officer whenever possible.

Hands on his hips, he scanned the room, taking in all the details he'd missed in the heat of the moment. The accommodations were clean and simple. A bed, computer console, a closet that held several suits similar to what Gar had been wearing earlier—nothing that screamed of extravagance. The room itself was in the interior of the ship, depriving him of even a view of the passing stars. Walking around though, he noticed the sheets on the bed were made with a natural fiber, not cheap synthetics. There was a personal datapad on the side table that contained several stories—fiction—and some had been marked as favorites. Gods, he was reading *Claxion Starburst*. Faolan wouldn't have thought Gar was that radical.

Then there were pictures.

Lined carefully along the back of a shelf, three onyx frames held the images of three separate groups of people. The first was a digital shot of an older man who looked to be in the middle of a heated conversation over a communicator. The image was most likely taken from a security camera, and Faolan had to wonder why Gar would have something like this. The second photo was on actual physical paper, singed around the corners and pressed carefully behind glass. The smiling couple was in stark contrast to the poor condition of the material. *Parents, maybe?* He could definitely see a resemblance.

The last picture—another paper photograph—was very blurry, to the point where neither of the faces were clearly visible. A young boy and girl, no older than ten or eleven, holding hands. They seemed to be running through a market, though Faolan couldn't tell if they were playing or being chased.

It was an odd assortment of memories, their significance apparent only to Gar.

A wave of dizziness sent Faolan stumbling to the bed. He sat on the mattress with a muffled *whoosh*, pressing a hand to his forehead as he waited for the sensation to pass. The spells were coming on more frequently and lasting longer. If he didn't get the medication soon, things would go badly for him far faster than he'd anticipated.

The stone was the key to everything. It wasn't tech, which made it a bit more challenging to convince people of its value, but once Krieg slipped it on, Faolan knew he could name his price. The money it would get him would more than support his crew for the next year and still give him the credits he needed. He just needed to convince Gar to trust him long enough to pull off the deal.

Ignoring an unexpected wave of guilt, he looked over to the bench built into the wall next to the bed and saw a neatly folded stack of clothing. He chuckled as he snatched the shirt from the top of the pile and pulled it over his head. The white fabric was soft against his skin, hugging his chest and sides. Clearly it belonged to Gar, who was slighter in stature than he but not by much. The pants were another matter. The material was too wide at the waist, sliding down to rest on his hips. Any running or twisting would send them falling to the floor. They couldn't belong to Gar; he'd never be able to keep them up. He slipped his own thick leather belt through the loops; it was a necessity rather than a fashionable adornment. All in all, not the best look on him, but with the whole begging-and-choosing predicament, he figured it would be in poor taste to argue.

Ignoring his boots for the time being, he padded quietly out into the hallway in search of his host. Not surprisingly, the door to engineering was locked, preventing him from taking a look at the engines. Gar wasn't stupid. The door across from the bedroom was also locked using both the DNA and security code to keep unwanted visitors out. He assumed it led to the cargo bay and cells.

As he approached the final set of doors, they slid open. His entrance was punctuated by a short blast of cool air. The room was so bright and clean it sparkled. A food preparation center from the look of it, one that Gar didn't use very frequently based on its pristine condition. Either that or his cleanliness tendencies were in serious need of being readjusted. How could anyone live like this?

Life was meant to be messy.

Eating, fighting, fucking—all of it got you out of the stagnant atmosphere and into the reality of living. It was clear to Faolan that, somewhere along the way, Gar had lost sight of the meaning of it all.

He needed to be reminded.

Checking the reading on the chronometer, he figured there was just enough time to make a quick meal before their next jump. Cooking was an indulgence he enjoyed, and he took pride in being able to spoil others with the fruits of his skills. Gar could stand a good meal, despite being in amazing shape. His pallor wasn't healthy.

Faolan wasn't surprised to find the ship's stores well stocked with space rations. And although the thin layer of dust on the containers did catch him off guard, it only served to reinforce his earlier suspicions. Slamming and banging around, he threw together a blend of ingredients—one of which looked to be some sort of meat—and waited on the dish as it simmered over the heating element. He was so engrossed in his task, he failed to notice Gar's arrival.

"What . . . in the gods' names . . . are you doing?"

He looked up and grinned. "Cooking."

Gar frowned. "Why?"

"I was hungry. Why else would I cook?"

"There is a perfectly good food replicator in the corner. This—" He waved his hand around in a wide, frantic circle. "This *mess* wasn't necessary."

Faolan snorted. "Of course it was. I can't make a proper meal without getting a few pots dirty. Trust me when I say you'll love it."

Gar moved into the room slowly. Faolan tried not to stare at him or give any indication just how sexy the rolled-up shirtsleeves looked on him. It also made Gar look relaxed in a way Faolan hadn't seen before now. It suited him.

Stopping a few feet shy of the cooking element, Gar rose up on the balls of his toes and peered into the pot. "What is it?"

"Doesn't have a name other than 'Faolan's Catchall.' My crew loves it, so it can't be too bad. Mind you, they only ever eat it when we're stuck dead in the middle of space, so it's not like they have many options."

"Poor them."

"You have no idea. Still, might want to consider trying it before you flush it out the airlock."

Holding up a spoonful, he waited to see if Gar would take the bait. Gar scrunched his nose but leaned forward and gave the contents a sniff.

"Spicy?"

"Can't handle it, bounty hunter?"

Gar rolled his eyes before opening his mouth and snatching up the sample. When Gar's eyes snapped wide open, Faolan chuckled and returned to his stirring. "See, it's worth it to try new things."

"That's good."

"I'm aware."

Grabbing two plates and filling them both, he didn't give Gar the option of turning down a meal. He shoved one into Gar's hand and made a point of ignoring him as he proceeded to stuff his mouth with food.

"You're going to choke if you don't slow down." Gar lifted a spoon and took a small bite.

"How long do we have until we hit the next dimension gate?"

"The ship will be in position in twenty minutes. I just came to make sure you were okay."

Faolan paused with his spoon halfway to his mouth. "Why wouldn't I be?"

"I thought you looked a little off earlier, is all."

"Rested and ready to go, Stitt. Once I finish eating, that is." He wasn't about to share anything more with Gar.

The silence that fell over the room had none of the awkwardness he normally experienced with people he'd slept with. It was also lacking the tension of their first encounter. As they stood eating, he noticed Gar would occasionally glance at him, only to look away when Faolan tried to catch his eye. They played that game until the food was nearly gone and Faolan had enough of the back and forth. He stared at Gar until the other man was blushing.

"What?" Gar poked a reconstituted vegetable with his spoon.

"What, *what*? You look like you have something you want to ask me."

"No. I don't."

Faolan huffed. "You're pissing me off, Stitt."

"It's just when you fell asleep, you went down hard. I couldn't move you."

Faolan stiffened. He knew he had nightmares, but normally he was wrung out after having suffered through a bout of them, and this morning he felt well rested. He didn't think it had to do with his lack of medication, which he wasn't about to bring up. "Well, that's not unusual for a sleeping man."

Gar shrugged. "Doesn't matter." He held up his now-empty plate and smiled. It wasn't the kind of grin Faolan would have expected, but something far more sincere. "Thanks for this."

"Least I can do. Consider it repayment for you not shooting my ass back on Tybal."

"About that—"

"Don't you dare. I set myself up to get caught. Just thought I'd have a chance to fuck someone before Krieg sent you to collect me."

Gar frowned but nodded, keeping his eyes averted. "Better get back to the cockpit. Need to make that jump soon. You'll want to brace yourself."

"Think you're going to leave me here to clean up the mess? I'll be right behind you."

Tossing the plates into the cleaning unit, the two men made their way to the front of the ship. Faolan felt himself relaxing for the first time in months, accompanying a man tasked with bringing him in if things went badly, no less. He couldn't put his finger on what it was about Gar that let him take the edge off and be himself. Certainly not Gar's reputation—he was no less a killer than Faolan.

More like they were kindred spirits who'd finally found each other.

"I promise the jump will be much smoother this time." Gar worked his sleeves down his arms as he lowered himself into the pilot's chair. "While you were resting, I took some time to make a few calibrations. No more banging your head."

"Thank the gods. I was going to complain to your boss."

Gar rolled his eyes, a reaction Faolan now realized was Gar's true personality coming through and not the image he wanted to project. Faolan liked it. It made him wonder what other idiosyncrasies the man had. It was almost a shame he wouldn't be around long enough to find out.

"Only two jumps after this until we get to my ship. Then you can see for yourself the power of this stone. Krieg will be all over me to have a chance to get it in his possession."

Gar turned his head, the look of relaxed amusement stripped from his face, replaced by an emotionless mask. He'd gone rigid in his seat.

"I'm sure he will. Please strap yourself in, Captain. We'll be jumping in a minute."

Faolan opened his mouth, but for once in his life he was at a total loss for what to say. It was like a cyber morphing blanket had been placed over Gar, completely changing his personality. The walls were back up, with no sight of the man he'd just shared a meal with.

He moved by rote and prepared for the jump. Why Gar's rapid personality change should bother him was a mystery. He wasn't here to make friends or find a life partner. This was about money, security, and his health, nothing more.

If Gar wanted to keep things professional, then he would too.

He took a deep breath and tried to relax his body as Gar tapped in the commands and maneuvered the *Geilt* where it needed to be. The guide beacons flashed red, then green before the computer chimed everything was ready.

"Dimension gate jump in three, two, one, jump."

The world shrank once again. No matter how many times Faolan lived through the event, there was something about a jump that made his head spin and his stomach flip. It wasn't normal, no matter how his medic tried to convince him otherwise. He'd gone so far as to ask Mace if she felt the same, but she'd simply rolled her eyes and called him a baby.

Maybe he was, but it still didn't feel *right*. It hadn't always been this way, which meant it was likely another symptom.

The ship lurched back into real space only moments after they'd left. He barely had time to blink before laser blasters pummeled the side of the *Geilt*.

"What the fuck!" Gar's shout echoed in the small space, but served the purpose of kicking him out of his thoughts. "Did you plan this, Wolf?"

"Like I'd set up the ship responsible for my safety. I'd have at least waited until I got myself off board." Faolan jumped forward and frantically typed a search command into the weapons grid. "Shit. I can't get a transponder signal on these bastards."

"Pirates?" Gar slammed the *Geilt* hard starboard and somehow managed to dodge a barrage of missiles.

"No one I know. Loyalists?"

"Probably." Gar growled, smashing his hand hard against the console. "Fuckers are jamming me."

"Shit." Faolan's mind raced as he tried to work out a plan. The *Belle Kurve* was too far away to be of any assistance, and if it really was a Loyalist attack crew, the authorities would be no good to them. "What region of the sector are we in?"

"Claxmont. Why?"

Shit, we might be able to pull this off and get out of here in one piece. "There is a planet near the edge of this system. It has five moons and a shitload of space debris. Head for it." He gave the coordinates.

Gar punched the numbers into the system. "What are you going to do?"

"Buy us some time. I hope. Weapons?"

"Laser cannon in the back and a pile of shields. I'm built for speed and stealth, not firepower."

"I could have told you that, darling." Faolan winked. "Be back soon."

Grabbing Gar's head, Faolan placed a sloppy, wet kiss on his cheek and dashed out of the room in the direction of engineering.

"I'll release the lock for you." Gar's voice was tinny over the ship's intercom. "Cannon room is the second door."

"Got it." Faolan prayed the few hours' rest he'd gotten would be enough to keep his eyesight sharp and his aim deadly. He really wished he'd put his boots on now.

The cannon controls were as basic as they came. A bank of monitors lined the small room, shouting out the array of the enemy fighters' approach vectors. Falling into the chair, he threw on the fire control visor and waited while his field of vision morphed into a three-dimensional view of the space around the outside of the ship. Computerized replicas of the enemy vessels buzzed in and out of his periphery, their image projections flickering slightly as the ships pitched and rolled.

"Okay, Gar, we've got five attackers on our tail. I'll lay down some cover fire for us until you can get me close to that debris."

"Then what?" It was odd hearing Gar's voice in his ears while looking out into the vastness of space.

"Then I'm going to blow some shit up."

"What?"

"There's *prymalin* in those rocks. They used to mine it in this sector before the big cache was found over near Veena." The ship shuddered. "Now stop talking and start flying!"

The *Geilt* listed hard to the starboard, bringing Faolan's cannon tracking in line with two of the other ships. He quickly got a lock on the closest one, sending a blur of lasers flying toward it. He landed a hit to that ship's front engine, halting its approach down to a crawl.

"I thought you liked the sound of my voice? One minute you're begging me to talk, the next you're telling me to shut up. Fickle, Captain?"

Faolan chuckled. "Note to self, Gar gets aroused and chatty when threatened. I pray to the gods I don't get trapped with you someplace we have to keep quiet."

A hard maneuver sent Faolan lurching in his chair. The back of his head was still a bit tender from the hit he'd taken in that earlier dimension jump, and the additional smack did little to improve the situation. Growling, he opened fire on the next ship, this time landing a direct hit on the shield generator and creating an explosion that ripped the enemy apart.

"I'm not *chatty*," Gar replied. "*Prymalin* field coming up. I'll open the throttle and swing below it. Should give you enough time to blow it, and for me to get my extra shielding in place."

"It will give them one hell of a light show. Let's just hope there's enough to blind them." Another barrage of shots.

"And not enough to blow us up in the process."

"Faith, Stitt. You need to have some. Go!"

The world spun around as Gar increased the engine thrust, causing the *Geilt* to fly forward. Nausea rolled through Faolan's stomach and forced him to close his eyes. *Shit, not now.* He sucked in several deep breaths, trying to keep the contents of his stomach down and hoping he could keep everything else together long enough to get them out of this alive.

"Faolan? We're almost through the field. Fire!"

Forcing his eyes wide, it only took a heartbeat for him to locate the largest of the derelict mining rocks, lock on with the cannon, and fire. There was a brief pause where nothing appeared to have happened, then a blinding light shot from within the rock, quickly chased by a spray of shards that ignited until the chain reaction filled the blackness of space.

For the few seconds he was able to see it, the riot of colors was the most amazing thing he'd witnessed in years. Regretfully, he closed his eyes and hoped there wouldn't be too much damage to his retinas. *Prymalin* burned brighter than any other substance known to man, and could easily blind a person if they weren't shielded properly. The poor bastards attacking them wouldn't stand a chance.

"You okay?" The note of concern in Gar's voice surprised him.

That remains to be seen. "Are you kidding? I'm fantastic. Swing us around and I'll get rid of these pests, then we can lie low for a bit."

There was a pause, and he could practically hear Gar's brain working overtime. "Fine. Get ready for the pass."

Faolan ignored Gar's annoyance and focused on the rapidly approaching ships. The remaining three were drifting, presumably due to the sudden blindness of their captains. After a few well-placed shots to disable their shields and engines, Gar and Faolan were free.

"Get us out of here, Gar. It won't take them long to get their scanners back online and start tracking us."

"I'll take us to one of the moons. We'll have to power down until the ship is ready to hit the next dimension gate."

Faolan pulled off the visor and rested his aching head gently against the seatback. His stomach still rolled from the ship's movement, and his head now throbbed with pain. The good periods between his symptoms were getting shorter and shorter, and that was if he didn't exert himself. He needed more rest, which was unlikely to happen given his current situation. Still, it couldn't hurt to take a few minutes for himself. Closing his eyes, he let out a soft huff and tried to gather his strength.

When a hand gently squeezed his shoulder, he jumped and knocked his attacker down. He leaped forward and pressed his forearm into the assailant's throat, pinning him to the floor before his brain caught up to what was happening.

"Faolan," Gar croaked out. "Let me go."

"Shit. *Shit.* Sorry."

He moved his arm away, but didn't get off Gar. Instead, he braced his hands on either side of Gar's head and fought to regain control through the sudden adrenaline rush. Gar didn't force him away. Instead he seemed content to watch Faolan, concern filling his eyes.

"You okay?" Gar asked softly. He pressed his palm against Faolan's cheek.

"Will be. Just closed my eyes for a second there. Didn't think I'd drifted."

"It was long enough that I got . . . well, you know." Gar chuckled. "Guess that'll teach me to sneak up on you. Eh, Wolf?"

Lying on top of Gar, looking down into those blue eyes, Faolan felt the now-familiar spark of attraction explode between them. The urge to lean forward and close the distance was too much for him to resist. Keeping his eyes open, he lowered his head just enough to brush his lips against Gar's. They were warm, moist, and tasted of iron. The side of his nose rubbed against Gar's as he pulled back, his skin tingling pleasantly in its wake. "You bit your lip."

"Nervous habit."

"Any other nervous habits I should be aware of?"

Gar smiled. It wasn't like any other Faolan had seen. This time Gar's eyes sparkled and the tension eased from his forehead and neck. "One or two. But I'll keep those to myself for the time being."

"I'll have to see if I can figure them out. I like challenges."

Placing another quick kiss on Gar's lips, he pushed himself to his feet before holding out a hand to help Gar up. Firm fingers squeezed until both men stood face-to-face once more. Their eyes locked for a moment before the ship quaked. A meteor bouncing off the shields, no doubt.

Gar recovered first, letting his bland mask fall back into place. "I left us drifting in orbit around the third moon. Best if we get back to the cockpit and hide the ship in a crater or in a sensor blind spot. Gods only know who attacked us."

"I imagine they won't give up that easily either. Lead the way."

"Can you get word to your crew? Tell them of the delay?"

The idea of breaking communication silence didn't sit well with him, but neither did the prospect of getting them blown the hell up. While there wasn't an immediate threat, he decided to play things safe. "They're running dark. No way of getting through."

Gar snorted. "I find that hard to believe. You have a backup plan for everything."

As they entered the cockpit, Faolan was about to retort when Gar stopped midstride. "What?"

"Shit."

"What?"

"I think ... No, it can't be."

"What?"

Gar ignored him as he strode over to the small computer panel along the side wall. Faolan listened to Gar's muffled curses in a language he could only assume was Zeten as Gar pulled up a stream of data from the ship. Frowning, he stepped beside Gar, letting his hand rest on the other man's shoulder.

"Are those readings from the attacking ships?"

"Bastard."

Faolan cocked an eyebrow. "Excuse me?"

"Jason. That fucking bastard!"

A very nasty realization hit Faolan. He knew the answer before he asked the question, could tell from the look of pure rage on Gar's face. Still, he needed to hear it, needed to be sure before he took any action.

"Tell me what those readings say."

Gar closed his eyes, the muscles in his jaw twitching from the pressure.

"They had Jason's transponder code buried in a layer of communications garble. I saw it when I was trying to get through the jamming, and I knew it was familiar, but I didn't think of it in the heat of the moment. I only now realized what it was and why I recognized it."

"Your boss tried to kill us?"

Gar opened his eyes and glared at Faolan. "He's a dead man."

CHAPTER

SEVEN

Gar had rolled up his sleeves and was now leaning shoulder-deep into the guts of the *Geilt*. Jason had sent a squad after him. *Him*! Those shots weren't intended to scare Faolan into trusting Gar—a tactic they'd used on more than one occasion—but had been designed to blow them both out of space.

"What the hell are you looking for again?"

Faolan had given up all pretense of helping about an hour ago and now stood propped against the wall, arms crossed and gaze fixed on Gar's ass—Gar had caught him staring more than once, and Faolan did nothing to hide his attentions, which wasn't improving Gar's mood.

Squeezing his eyes shut, he silently counted to ten before standing straight and flashing Faolan a fake smile. "As I said, I'm looking for the tracker Jason put on my ship."

"Ah, right." Faolan toyed with his chin. "And how do you know there is a tracker? I wouldn't think you'd let anyone near your baby."

He wouldn't. Not normally. No one other than prisoners and dead bodies were brought on board. Certainly no one was allowed to roam the halls. Faolan had been the one and only exception.

"It's the only way for him to have found us. It's not like I had the coordinates prior to you giving them to me."

"Not a chance he could have intercepted, oh, I don't know, a transmission of the coordinates, say from your computer?"

Gar's already fragile hold over his temper shattered. He threw the electro-mag wrench against the wall and strode over to where the pirate stood. "What the hell is that supposed to mean? Are you accusing me of something, Wolf?"

Faolan held his hands up in mock surrender, but Gar could tell he was anything but intimidated. Anger floated beneath the surface of Faolan's easygoing exterior, and Gar knew it would take very little to push the captain over the edge.

"I'm not accusing you of anything, Stitt. I just find the whole situation a bit . . . *peculiar*."

"Jason tried to kill me. I really don't give a shit what you think. What I need to figure out is how he tracked me so I can find the bastard without him knowing I'm on the way."

Faolan didn't move, his appraising gaze taking inventory of Gar's reaction. Gar really didn't care *what* the pirate thought of him. They were just stuck together until Gar could dump his ass somewhere and go after Jason. Shit, it would mean he'd have to go back to Zeten. His home world held very few good memories for him.

Faolan shrugged and lowered his arms. "You might want to ask why Jason would try to kill one of the guild's best bounty hunters. You're not the type of asset anyone would want to lose. What it means is the stakes are a hell of a lot higher than you thought they were."

"It doesn't matter. He betrayed me." The one man he trusted with his life had tried to end it. "No one does that and lives to tell the story."

Faolan nodded once, understanding clear on his face. "Remind me never to piss you off."

"You wouldn't live long enough for the reminder to stick."

Smiling, Faolan pushed away from the wall and sauntered past him to the engine. "My earlier question still stands. How did someone get inside to place a tracker here? Wouldn't an external one be easier?"

"Not with my shields. They're passive-defensive when I'm in dock. A simple touch to the outside is fine, but if you try to attach something to the hull, you get zapped. The shields send out short-range, targeted EMP too. It disables anything electronic not flagged with my ship's signature within a certain radius." He paused. "No, the only way a tracker got on this ship is from the inside. Someone came into my ship and placed it here."

"You think Krieg managed to do that when you weren't looking?"

It was hard to believe. He had always prided himself on the level of security of the *Geilt*—been obsessive about it if he was being honest. Jason had teased him more than once about his fussy nature.

Sneaking a tracker into his home and rubbing his nose in it was certainly something Jason would do. Incentive enough for Faolan . . . and if Gar blew up along with the *Geilt*, he wouldn't even be around to collect payment for the job, which would have been convenient for Jason. That still left the question of *why* Jason wanted Gar dead, though.

"I was on Tybal Station longer than anticipated. My information wasn't as clear as it normally is. If he'd managed to get my security codes, it wouldn't have taken an operative long to get on board and place it. I have a normal maintenance schedule and wouldn't have looked for anything before then."

Faolan leaned over the engine, locked his hands behind his back and peered inside. "You're a slave to routine. Krieg took advantage because he knows you so well."

Suddenly tired, Gar scrubbed a hand down his face and pressed his back against the wall, sliding down until his ass touched the floor and he could rest his forearms on his knees. "I'm an idiot."

"No, you're not. You made a mistake in trusting someone. Means you're human after all, Stitt. Flawed and fucked up like the rest of us."

Human, yes, but Jason had been like a father to him. Gar had spent the better part of the last ten years doing everything in his power to please the man. He'd come close to turning into the kind of person he hated. Every day he fought the urge to go that step too far, take more than he should, hurt others just a little bit too much. He would walk up to the invisible edge he'd drawn in the sand, only to stand there and stare at it.

He wasn't like them, the men who'd killed his family.

Gar closed his eyes and did his best to ignore the darkness threatening to eat him alive, inside out. He couldn't do this on his own anymore. "I still can't believe he would do this to me."

"Well, life is designed to challenge our perceptions. If it doesn't, we never learn and grow. We also can never recognize what a Damasmus tracking beacon looks like."

Gar's head snapped up from where it rested on his knees. "You found something?"

Faolan was shoulders-deep inside the maintenance port Gar had abandoned.

"Aha!" He surfaced holding a small silver component that looked strangely like a Zeten sand spider. "Look at that beauty. My dear Mr. Stitt, I would like to introduce you to your unwanted tracker."

Jason really did try to have him killed. "Bastard."

"Want me to smash this little shit?"

Plans whizzed through his mind—everything from smashing it and disappearing forever to placing it on a garbage barge to wait for Jason's men to show up. "Not yet. We're lucky this planet is causing problems with the signal. It will give us some time to come up with a plan. We can use it to throw him off the scent before we're ready to get to your ship."

Faolan grinned. "Sneaky. I like it."

"Thought you would." Gar pushed himself up, brushing invisible dust from his pants. "I have an escape pod we can stick it on and send through the dimension gate. Should keep him running in circles for a little bit at least."

"As long as he doesn't send anyone to come collect us in the meantime, we'll be good." Faolan tossed the tracker to him. "We'll need to move quickly. How much longer does the ship need before she can jump?"

Gar looked at the chronometer ticking down on the monitor. "Not long. Twenty minutes."

"Just long enough for us to get the pod ready." Faolan grinned and started to stride past. "Let's get moving, then."

He'd almost made it past Gar when he stumbled, as if he'd tripped over his own feet. Gar's arm flew out to catch him around the waist, pulling Faolan in tight against his side.

"Let go," Faolan snapped. "I'm fine."

"Your legs gave out."

"I tripped. Just clumsy."

Gar huffed out a breath. "Wolf, I've known you for two days now, and prior to that spent a hell of a lot of time reading your file. 'Clumsy' isn't a word I'd use to describe your sorry ass. What the hell is going on?"

A blush dusted Faolan's cheeks. "There's nothing wrong. Just didn't get enough rest."

"You slept for over ten hours. How is that not enough?"

Faolan straightened and pushed away. Gar immediately missed his warmth, but did nothing to stop him. Faolan didn't meet his gaze; instead, he set about tucking the hem of the shirt into his low-riding pants.

"Some days I need more than average. Don't let yourself think there is something wrong with me. I can kill you faster than your average space pirate and still make it back to my ship in time for last meal."

Gar recognized the dismissive tone as one he used himself on many occasions. It shouted to the world that while yes, there clearly was a problem, he wasn't about to air it to everyone so kindly back the hell off.

"Would never question it, Wolf."

Faolan straightened. "Good. Now let's get that tracker to the pod so we can find my ship. I'm dying for some real clothing."

"Got a problem wearing my stuff?" Gar snorted and tried to act casual even though he made sure to keep close to Faolan as they made their way through the ship. "I'll have you know that shirt cost me two hundred credits and is handmade."

"The pants are a bit big though."

Gar nodded, but wasn't about to admit they'd belonged to his father. "Wasn't going to give you the good ones."

"At least I know where you spend all your money. Should have guessed it was on your clothing."

The idea that Faolan had put any thought at all into his monetary habits was interesting in itself. "Where did you think I was spending it?"

"Until I came on board, I would have said booze or drugs. No one leads as clean a life as you appeared to."

Given the image he'd taken great pains to cultivate, it wasn't surprising to realize others would imagine he had a much darker side than even what he showed the world. He didn't—he couldn't afford to be weak, not when he was still on the hunt for the man who'd destroyed his family, murdered his father. Someday he'd find the bastard and when he did, Gar would tear his world apart.

"Pretty boring, I am. You're far more interesting, Wolf."

"You don't know the half of it." Faolan stopped once they reached the secondary passage that led to the escape pods. "You want to lead the way? Unless you want me to crack a few of your codes, in which case, I'm game."

Gar shouldered his way ahead and was about to type in the security code when he paused. "Actually, would you?"

Faolan frowned. "What?"

"Hack in?"

"Seriously?"

Gar let his hand fall to his side and did his best to ignore the confusing stir of emotions—his need for revenge mixed with a desire to have Faolan close. Swallowing, he swayed closer to Faolan, enjoying the proximity. "Someone broke through my defenses. The only way I can fix it, make it stronger, is to have someone try to replicate what was done. If you can hack in and tell me how to fix my security, I'd . . ."

Faolan waited for a moment before he pressed his shoulder against Gar's back. "You'd be what? Grateful? Need to pay back my kindness? I remind you that you still owe me a debt, bounty hunter. You don't want to rack too many up, or I may just steal you away."

Gar looked up and couldn't stop the small smile from slipping across his face. "I'd appreciate it."

They stood there until Faolan broke out in a grin. "Careful, Stitt. I have a feeling we might be moving away from a hunter and mark relationship and becoming dangerously close to friends."

"Not possible. I've only known you two days."

"You wouldn't be the first to be wooed by my charm, wit, and devastating good looks."

Gar rolled his eyes. "No fear of that happening."

Faolan stepped back, cracking his knuckles. "Give me room, kid. Let me show you what a professional scoundrel can do."

Instantly regretting the decision to let this happen, Gar bowed deeply at his waist and swept his arm wide in invitation. Faolan didn't press any of the buttons immediately, instead he leaned forward to inspect the panel.

"Third tier . . . bio lock . . . three years old . . ." Faolan dropped to his knees to gain access to the control panel beneath the console.

A gentle press against the corner of the metal made the hatch pop open, exposing the vibrant colors of the circuitry.

"That came off with disturbing ease." Gar tried to move closer to get a better look. "How did you learn to do that?"

"You're in my light, Stitt."

Gar jerked up and back. "Sorry."

Faolan looked at him and winked. "Just trying to impress you with my speed."

"I'd rather go for quality."

"Everyone's a critic." Faolan let out a sharp bark of laughter as he pulled a small electrode from a hidden compartment of his belt. "Now if I just put this here . . ."

The door beeped mournfully twice before it slid open. Gar shook his head. "I don't believe it."

"Hacked in less than two minutes. I'm getting rusty. I used to be able to crack any third-tier security system in thirty seconds."

Gar pinched the bridge of his nose. "I guess it's safe to say, then, the *Geilt* was compromised by a pro."

"Yeah, sorry. The good news is there are only a few people who would have a clear understanding of your system, so that should help you narrow it down. It really is quite effective."

"Didn't look like it from where I was standing."

Faolan placed a hand on Gar's shoulder. Warmth from the touch seeped through his shirt, tempting him to move against Faolan. The space between them heated as Faolan smiled, leaning forward close enough to speak in nothing more than a soft whisper.

"I have yet to meet anything that can keep me out. Don't think there's anything wrong with your ship. Your average hacker would have either needed an hour to do what I just did or someone to hand them the ship schematics."

"No one has those. I wiped them from the space dock's central computer after I took possession of the *Geilt*." Gar swallowed. "And you're far from average."

He'd intended it to have come out as a question, but knew it hadn't. A flare of lust flashed between them, sending electricity crackling along his skin. He didn't resist as Faolan shoved him against the wall next to the open door. Hot air caressed his neck. Faolan's lips moved close to his face. Gar's body was ahead of his brain, cock already half-hard in his pants. Gods, he wanted this—he needed to be with someone he could talk to, who would listen to him, who wouldn't let him surrender to the darkness threatening to consume him. Faolan could be that man.

"You know, Gar, you're nowhere near the norm either. There's something about you . . . You feel it too, right? This *thing*?" Faolan pressed his hand to Gar's sternum, only to flex his fingers, digging into the material of his shirt. "I know you do."

Gar reached up, clutched Faolan's arms, and prayed the sudden spinning of his world would stop. "Not the best time for this."

Faolan nipped at his neck. "Never a bad time for this."

"Jason is tracking us and we are floating in space like a practice target. He'll send more ships once he realizes we're still alive."

"And as soon as we release it, they will be off chasing your escape pod in some random corner of the galaxy."

"Faolan."

"Shut up, Gar. Just . . . shut up."

Gar arched his neck back and to the side, giving Faolan complete access, silently begging him to do *something*. Faolan hummed low and deep in his throat as he latched on to the juncture of Gar's shoulder with a playful bite.

"I want to fucking devour you." Faolan licked a wet trail up to Gar's ear. He flicked the lobe with his tongue. "I want to hear you beg me to fuck you. I want you to cry because I made you come so hard you saw stars."

Gar shivered. "No."

"Oh yes. You'll want me. You'll be panting for it, in fact. And I'll deliver, but not before I have you on all fours and pleading for me to take you. You'd like that, wouldn't you?"

Yes, gods, yes. "No, I've never let . . . No one has ever—"

Faolan's head snapped up. "You mean you've *never*, not once?"

Heat flushed across Gar's face. "Don't think I'm about to let you either."

"Oh baby, don't lay that kind of challenge at my feet and expect me to back down. I'll have you begging for my cock up your ass in no time."

Gar braced his hands against Faolan's shoulders and shoved hard. "I don't think so, and I'm not your fucking 'baby.'"

Faolan chuckled as he rubbed the skin through his shirt. "No? How about 'sugar'? 'Sweetie'? 'Honey'?"

"Bastard, pirate."

Gar marched away, adjusting the bulge in his pants en route to the escape pod. How the hell did he let himself get sucked into Faolan's charms like that? He didn't need to have someone fret over him like a child or some fragile lover. He had been on his own since he escaped Zeten when he was fourteen and had been doing fine on his own. He never let himself be vulnerable, let someone have control over him, or ever put his needs in the hands of anyone. The last time he trusted anyone, his father and sister had paid the price, and now this thing with Jason— *Never again.*

"Gar."

He could handle his demons on his own. He'd been just fine before Faolan showed up, he'd be just as good when he left.

"Gar, wait."

Gods, he needed this to be over so he could get Faolan to his ship and slip away to some nebula where he could plan his revenge. With Jason's betrayal apparent, Gar would go to other places and people who would be more than happy to pay a fair price for his services. Places where he would be safe when the guild came after him for eventually taking Jason out.

"Gar!"

"Once I install this on the escape pod, we'll make the next jump. Then you can contact your ship and arrange pickup." His life would get back to normal soon enough. Gar just needed to live through the next few days.

One day. He could do this.

"Will you *wait*?"

He stopped short and spun on his heel. Faolan wasn't expecting it and stumbled, nearly crashing into him. The surprised look on Faolan's face would have been amusing if Gar wasn't as angry as he was.

"Look, Wolf, just forget about it. Despite what you think, there is nothing here. You were a mark I had to bring in. I should have killed you on the spot and saved myself a shitload of headaches. Instead, the man I thought of as another father just tried to have me killed, and you want me to lie down and let you take advantage of me. Well, fuck that and fuck you. We are going to place this tracker on an escape pod, launch it into the next sector, jump, and call your ship. This time one day from now, I expect you to be so far away from me I won't remember your face. Understand?"

Whatever emotion was on Faolan's face faded into nothing the moment the final word left Gar's mouth. To say Faolan's face was blank wasn't entirely accurate. He was clearly trying to work out the best thing to say. What Gar wasn't expecting was the sincerity behind the words when Faolan finally spoke.

"What did they do to you to make you so scared?"

Rage and indignation fired Gar's blood, but he couldn't voice it. He *was* scared—terrified if he was willing to admit it. His whole life he'd run from the comfort basic human connections offered him. Every single person he'd ever loved had been stripped from his life in one way or another. He wasn't willing to risk his heart again, no matter who was the offered prize.

Ignoring the pounding of his heart, he clenched his teeth. "One day. Then either your ship gets you or you can wait, floating in space in an EV suit."

Faolan's eyes bored into his, but he didn't say anything else. A single nod was the only confirmation Gar received.

"Then let's get to work," Gar ground out before turning and marching away.

CHAPTER
EIGHT

Faolan had encountered many crazy and fucked-up people in his life, but no one as much so as Gar Stitt. Sure, he could completely understand the man's reluctance to spread his legs and let Faolan fuck him. It wasn't an easy thing to let another person take control like that, even if that other person was one fantastic lover. What could he say that wouldn't sound like a pathetic attempt to woo Gar? Not a whole hell of a lot.

A change in tactics was required.

When a direct attack didn't work, often the best course of action was to avoid the situation and work with more subtle undertones. Gar was scared. Gar wasn't used to someone else being in control. Gar was a stuck-up ass who needed to relax before his head exploded.

Faolan wanted to be the one to help him.

Which was why he had to be smart about his next move. Too much and Gar would shoot him. Too little and he would simply ignore the offer Faolan was waving in front of his face. Maybe he could split the difference and hit Gar over the head.

"Pass me the transceiver." He held out his hand and waited for Gar to respond. He didn't look at him, no matter how much he wanted to stare at the way the muscles moved in Gar's forearm.

"How much longer?" Gar's voice was soft, the words the most he'd spoken since their blowup.

Faolan had no idea he'd missed the sound of another person's voice, but gods that was the sweetest noise he'd heard all day. "I'll be done once I get this put in. Then off it goes."

"Then off we go."

The unspoken *off you go* wasn't lost on him. Gods, it pissed him off he couldn't break through Gar's protective shell. He *liked* the Zeten. He had *never* met a Zeten he could tolerate for more than ten minutes, let alone want to fuck his brains out. With the exception of Mace, but she was a completely different scenario. Hell, she didn't even have the accent anymore. The silent ticking of time flying forward wasn't helping matters. He had less than one day to win Gar over before the *Belle Kurve* arrived to whisk him away, allowing Gar to disappear forever into the black of space.

Slapping his hands on his thighs, he stood up to crack the vertebrae in his back. "Done. Guaranteed you won't find a better quality job or your credits back."

Gar nodded and moved to the escape pod. Faolan didn't shift away from the computer panel, wanting Gar to either make him move or brush up against him. He almost laughed out loud at the look of annoyed frustration when Gar realized what he was doing. Instead of saying anything at all, Gar walked around to the other side and accessed the secondary navigation system. *Mark one for the bounty hunter.*

"What sector would be the best to send the pod?" Gar quirked an eyebrow. "We don't want to set it too close to your ship."

"Don't you worry about my ship. My crew can more than handle anything Krieg throws at them." Sauntering around the pod, Faolan shoved his hands in his pants pockets and tried to keep his casual air. "Where would you hide your ship if you were looking for a safe harbor?"

He watched Gar chew his bottom lip. *Another glimpse of Gar the man.* "Why?"

"Well, this is supposed to be you, right? Only makes sense you should pick a spot where you'd normally hide, considering Krieg would try to anticipate what you would do. Anything less will look suspicious."

Gar considered this, all while his fingers beat out a nervous tattoo against the escape pod. "Tridan Nebula. It's a conceivable place for me to hide and it has lots of debris I would be able to use as weapons or shields. Plus there are several sensor blackout areas I would use to my advantage."

Faolan stopped a generous foot away from Gar's back, nodding his head in agreement even though he knew he wasn't completely visible. "Then the Tridan Nebula it is."

Without waiting for Gar to respond, he strode out of the workroom and made his way toward the kitchen. Pleased he'd sufficiently unnerved Gar, Faolan planned to make the most of his strategic retreat. There was a particularly comfortable chair he'd spotted earlier he wanted to test out, and he needed to rest if he didn't want to alert Gar to the fact he really *wasn't* completely all right.

The door to the kitchen was in sight before Gar's footsteps finally echoed behind him. "Hey!"

Faolan slowed but didn't stop. "Problem?"

"Where are you going?" Gar stopped him with a hand on his shoulder.

He let Gar hold him, ignoring the rush of blood down to his cock. "Kitchen. Thought I'd grab something quick to eat, unless you plan on starving me for the next day."

"Don't you need to contact your ship?" Gar had lowered his voice, gently squeezing Faolan. "Let them know about the danger?"

Gods, his touch was perfect. Before he realized what he was doing Faolan covered Gar's hand with his own and returned the squeeze. "We have a plan worked out. They'll wait for me only so long, then they'll head to our backup rendezvous."

"I . . . I'm glad. Hate the idea of anyone suffering because of what I've done."

Faolan turned to face Gar, comforted when he didn't pull his hand away. "How is it your fault? I seem to remember being the one who set himself up as bait in a bar waiting for Krieg to send his goons. No offense."

"None taken. It still doesn't explain why he'd want to kill me."

The urge to wrap Gar in a hug was odd but powerful. "Gods only know what is driving that crazy ass at the moment. We'll figure it out, and when we do, I'll help you disappear for a bit if you want."

Gar stepped back, his hand floating in the air until gravity kicked in and it drifted down to his side. "Why would you want to help me? After everything, me trying to kill you . . . Why?"

Faolan frowned. "Does it matter?"

"Yes."

The emphatic way Gar said it sent a shiver through Faolan. "You seem to have gone through an awful lot in your life, and yet you're still your own man. You could have killed me on sight like Krieg ordered you to and collected the bounty."

"How do you know Jason—"

Faolan moved closer to Gar again, mildly surprised when Gar backed away until he was pressed against the wall. He didn't touch Gar, but stayed close enough to see the muscles in his neck tighten.

"I've gotten pretty good at reading people. Had to, given my line of work. The first thing I figured out when I saw you was how tight you keep everything wrapped up. You don't let people in, no matter what is going on in that handsome head of yours. The only problem with not letting people in is that one day, when your world collapses under the weight of all your problems and issues, there's no one to help you."

Gar's breathing was heavy, his pupils blown wide despite the stiffness with which he held his body. "In the end we're all alone anyway."

"Doesn't mean you can't fight against it, grab and hold on to the things that are important to you and don't let go. If things change, you change. You can't make decisions about your future that way. Don't give up on living before you've had a chance to experience it for real."

Gar let out a strangled growl and shoved him away. "I've experienced enough shit in my life. I don't *want* to invite more."

Faolan braced himself for the attack he knew would follow. "You're fucking useless, Stitt. There are people out there you could be helping, but you're too afraid to do something about it."

Gar's fist connected with his jaw, jerking him off-balance, but not enough to knock him down. He rubbed the throbbing skin and chuckled. "That's it? I thought you were some tough-ass bounty hunter—"

Gar leaped on him, the unexpected weight toppling them both to the floor. He managed to land a punch to Gar's stomach before Gar continued his assault. The rage and pain on Gar's face was clear, the grimace distorting his normally passive expression into an accurate image of what he was feeling. Faolan groaned as Gar grabbed his head and slammed it against the floor.

"Stop." The protest was weak, but it was all Faolan could manage.

"I never asked you to come here and tear things apart. You were a bloody mark!"

"Gar . . . stop."

Gar landed another punch, this time to Faolan's side. "I'm not supposed to like you."

Blackness crept across Faolan's vision, making everything fuzzy. "Gar . . ."

He must have lost consciousness, because the next thing he realized he was being dragged down the ship's corridor. "Fuck."

"Faolan?" Gar set him down flat before flying to his side. "I'm so sorry. Gods, are you okay?"

If it hadn't been for the fact Gar had just beaten him senseless, he would have found the expression of worry and regret slightly amusing. Even in his current state he would have normally made some sort of smart-ass remark to take the edge off the situation.

He couldn't.

Tears rolled down Gar's cheeks in two streams, but he gave no indication he even knew they were present. Faolan reached up and brushed his thumb across them, wanting to ease Gar's pain. "I'm okay."

Gar shook his head. "You're not. I beat you *unconscious*. I never . . . I'm not . . ." Gar squeezed his eyes shut. "I'm so, *so* sorry."

Faolan might have been dying, but he could still handle a beating. "I'm okay. Gar, look at me."

Gar scrunched his face up like a child and shook his head again. "I'm not like them. I don't cross the line. You made me cross the line, and . . . I was angry. But I'm not like them. I promised myself I would never go that far."

Faolan's heartbeat raced. He swallowed and slid his hand around to the back of Gar's neck. "I know you're not like them. Gar, look at me." He made sure to use the same tone he did when his ship was under attack.

It worked. Gar slowly relaxed his face and opened his eyes. Gone was the cocky bounty hunter who'd blazed across the galaxy doing the will of the guild. All Faolan was able to see was a scared and lonely young man who'd spent far too many years dealing with shit on his own. Ignoring the throbbing in his head, he pulled Gar down and brushed a gentle kiss across his lips.

"You're not like them, whoever hurt you. If you were, you'd be dumping my body out an airlock instead of taking me . . . Where the hell were you dragging me?"

Gar let out a short laugh, surprising them both. "My room, to get you fixed up."

"Don't you have a med bay?"

"I converted it into a holding cell. Figured I was the only one I'd ever need to heal up and I'd much rather be in my own bed than on one of those cots."

In a sad sort of way, it made sense. "Help me up. I think I can walk the rest of the distance on my own."

Gar was on his feet and helping him without hesitation. Considering what had happened, Faolan was surprisingly steady. With any luck that meant no concussion. Gar latched on to his waist and kept him close as they moved. He really could have made it on his own, but knew Gar needed the physical reassurance that he was okay.

The kid could throw one hell of a punch.

"I have a scanner we can use to check out your head. To make sure I didn't do any permanent damage to that thick skull of yours."

Faolan grinned. "You wouldn't be the first person to try and to fail."

Gar grimaced. "I'm just sorry to be on the list at all."

"I'm not." Faolan kept his gaze straight ahead as they moved, ignoring Gar's confused stare. "It just means when I collect on our earlier bet, I get to be a little rougher on you."

Gar sighed. "I'm being serious."

"So am I! You think I'm going to give up on the opportunity to make you do whatever I want? Please. I thought you'd gotten to know me pretty well over the past couple days."

The door to Gar's room slid open after Gar released the security lock. The sheets were still rumpled from earlier that day. The mess didn't undermine the appeal of the bed in the least.

"Gods, I need to get one of these on my ship."

"Worth every credit. Now let's get you horizontal before you pass out and I have to drag your worthless body again."

"We need to work on your bedside manner, doctor."

He didn't let go of Gar's body when he sat on the bed, pulling Gar with him. Instead of hard metal, the soft support of the mattress caught them, allowing them to tangle in a pleasant heap.

Wrapping his arm around Gar's neck, Faolan held him still. "We have time."

"Faolan—"

"We have time before my ship arrives where it needs to be to pick us up."

"Jason and his men—"

"Fine." Faolan released him and rolled onto his back. "Send the escape pod through the dimension gate and get us someplace safe. Don't expect me to help."

"Faolan, you're being childish."

"And you sound like my late wife." He froze the second he realized what he'd said. The information itself wasn't what was unnerving, but rather the idea he hadn't thought anything of saying it to Gar. Very few knew of Kayla and what had happened to her. It wasn't a conversation piece he normally spit out, especially lying in someone's bed. A quick glance at Gar and Faolan caught him rolling his eyes.

"I feel for anyone who had to put up with you."

He tried to stop the chuckle, but couldn't. "You're no space walk either, starshine."

Gar's smile was quick, but no less present. He tapped his fingertip to the middle of Faolan's chest. "Are you sure you're okay?"

Like he was about to tell the truth on that one. "All engines fired and ready to go."

"Good. I'm going to finish programming the escape pod for its journey and send it on its way. Then we'll need to hide a bit deeper in a low orbit for a day. Only way to be sure Jason has taken the bait and can't hack into the gate systems to see where we've really gone."

"What can I do to help?"

Gar remained still, but Faolan could practically hear the gears in his head spinning. After a moment, Gar moved forward and pressed a kiss to his temple. "Nothing. Wait here and I'll be back soon. Think of ways for me to make things up to you."

Faolan shivered, and his voice shook as he spoke. "Prepare yourself if you're handing me a charged laser like that. I'm not afraid to use it."

"It's no less than I deserve. Be back soon. You rest."

"I can help."

"I know, but it will only take me a few minutes. When I get back, I'll throw myself at your mercy."

Faolan was still staring at the closed door several minutes after Gar had left. Cursing when he realized what he was doing, he rolled onto his side and did his best to think up punishments. It was then he saw one of Gar's ties curled on top of the desk. Ties. Tied up.

Perfect.

He moved around the room far more slowly than normal, but better than he expected given recent events. It meant he would be strong enough to do what he wanted to do to Gar, even if he had to take things at a more sedate pace. Mace always said he needed to work on his patience. It didn't take him long to find the items he wanted and shove them under the pillow. Then he stripped his borrowed clothing away, tossing the pile in a corner. He'd worry about wrinkles later.

The *Geilt* trembled as he climbed naked along the bed. Gar's voice crackled through the com system. "I just released the escape pod. It should reach the gate in twenty minutes. I'm going to lower the ship in orbit now, so there might be some hull stress until I stabilize us."

Faolan pressed the com button on the wall behind the bed. "Just don't take us too low and crush this rust bucket in the upper atmosphere."

"I'm going to smack your ass for that comment."

"Not tonight, Stitt. I'm calling the shots, remember?" Silence greeted him, which only made him smile more. For good measure, he reached over and hit the com again. "Speaking of which, make sure you are mostly naked when you get in here. I have lost time to make up for."

He didn't think Gar would respond at all, so he was surprised when a husky "Yes, sir" crackled over the speaker. The words weren't careless or casual—Gar was clear in what he was offering.

Oh fuck.

His cock ached as it pressed up against his stomach, leaking pre-cum. The mere thought of Gar being submissive to him, getting on his knees, begging, and waiting for him to grant or withhold pleasure, made him ache. *Gar* was willing to do this. He knew the bounty hunter didn't go down this road normally. There was something between them that made this whole situation more bizarre, more sweet.

Gods, what was happening to him? How could he grow so attached to someone after only a couple of days?

The urge to jerk off before Gar arrived was strong, but he held back. While it would do wonders for his stamina, if he was going to make Gar suffer, then it was only fair to wait until he could show his appreciation appropriately.

Plans unfolded in his mind, each successive one more elaborate, each new position more enticing than the last. If Gar didn't get in here soon, there would be no hope for either of them. The silent summons was heeded as the door slid open with a *whoosh*.

Gar stood in the entrance, shirt unbuttoned and free from his pants. His sleeves were undone too, the cuffs flopping wide. The black belt Faolan had admired earlier was now gone, as were his shoes and socks. Gar didn't smirk or give any indication of fear or reluctance as he stepped inside, letting the door close behind him.

"Took you long enough," Faolan said softly, pillowing his hands behind his head. "Good boy for listening."

He saw the muscle in Gar's jaw jump. No doubt he'd bitten back one of his normal retorts. Faolan knew this would be hard for Gar to play along, so he didn't want to push things too much this time.

However, next time . . .

"Come to the side of the bed, but don't get on it."

Gar moved easily, the fabric of his pants hugging his hips low as he moved. Faolan watched a blush bloom on Gar's chest and travel up across his skin until it reached his throat. The sight was beautiful.

"The bet was the loser had to do whatever the winner wanted without protest."

"That wasn't what you said."

Faolan cocked an eyebrow. "Reneging on your deal?"

Gar growled. "Not at all."

"Good, because I've had lots of time to plan things out for us. Trust me when I say it will be worth the effort."

Faolan waited until Gar nodded before continuing. "Come here. Get on the bed and lean over me, but no touching."

This time there was no hesitation. Gar climbed onto the bed easily, letting his feet hang over the side. Leaning forward, he braced a hand on either side of Faolan's head and looked down into his eyes. Right then and there, Faolan almost gave up the game and let his impulses take over. He shivered as Gar's hot breath tickled his now-cool skin.

No, he had to do this right. They both deserved it.

Looking directly into Gar's eyes, Faolan smiled.

"I want you to tell me that I can do whatever I want to you. And I want you to mean it."

CHAPTER

NINE

For a moment, Gar thought his cock would explode, it grew so hard. Of all the lovers he'd had over the years, never had anyone taken control. He knew part of the appeal of being with him was his dominant streak. Women loved it. The men he'd bedded never seemed to complain, even seemed to enjoy their brief power struggles.

He always won in the end.

Not this time.

With Faolan, it wasn't up for discussion. Faolan was taking the lead, no room for argument. Certainly Gar had the option to say no on the participation side of things, step away without pressure. For the first time, he was okay with someone else looking after *his* needs. He was tired of always being at someone's beck and call.

If he stopped to put any thought into why he was able to go down this route with Faolan and not with any of the others, he wasn't sure what he'd find. The connection was there, the raw spark of lust tinged with want and, surprisingly, trust, setting his blood on fire. There was more to it than attraction. One look into Faolan's eyes and Gar knew he cared—not only about his physical pleasure, but about Gar's other desires. Faolan clearly recognized the darkness swirling deep inside his being, and refused to back down. He was willing to lift the burden from Gar's shoulders, even if it was only a temporary respite, which was more than anyone had ever done for him.

The simple act had his heart aching for more.

Opening his mouth to speak the words was still hard, no matter how much he wanted to say them. Darting his tongue out to spread moisture across his bottom lip, he kept his gaze on Faolan. He could do this—wanted to do this for both their sakes. Anticipation was clear on Faolan's face as the pirate gently bucked his hips up into the air.

"Gar, I need you to say it. I know you well enough now to realize you won't relax and enjoy this if you don't." Faolan reached up and traced a line down the middle of his chest with a single finger. "Give it up to me. Say it."

Gods, I'm so screwed. "You can do—" he sucked in a deep breath, ignoring a flash of panic "—anything you want to me."

Faolan didn't pounce on him like he expected. Instead, Faolan offered him a gentle smile that shone in his eyes. "Very good. I promise you won't regret it. Now . . ." He flicked the hanging edge of Gar's shirt away. "As much as I like this look on you, I want you to sit up and take it off. Let me see you this time."

Exhibitionism was never something Gar got a thrill from. He'd spent his entire life running or hiding—most of the time with his life in danger. Putting his naked body on display for his lover was a risky move and far beyond the controlled, quick fucks he'd had in the past. Slowly, careful not to go too fast and freak himself out, he sat back on his legs so he loomed over Faolan's naked body. With no barriers to draw the process out, he easily shrugged one shoulder, then the other, to let gravity pull the cloth down until it was trapped at his wrists. Stretching his arms behind his body allowed the shirt to drop to the floor while the muscles of his arms and chest grew taut.

Faolan's cock twitched as he bucked his hips once more. "Very nice. I want you to touch yourself. Run your fingers through your chest hair and play with your nipples."

"Didn't know it was my turn to put on a show." He shifted his hand, gaining more confidence with each passing second.

"You're doing whatever I want you to. If that means giving me a show, then so be it. Pinch them."

He closed his eyes, but followed Faolan's command. He couldn't stop the gasp at the overpowering sensation his touch produced. An invisible thread from the nipple to his cock pulled with every flick and roll of his fingers. He didn't think as he reached down to touch his shaft, needing to stroke it through his pants.

"Don't you dare!"

Gar jumped, and his eyes flew open. "What?"

Faolan leaned up on his arms and glared. "You were going to touch your cock and that is against the rules."

The hard set of Faolan's jaw and the intensity of his gaze told Gar how seriously he was taking the game. Here was the leader Gar had read about in Faolan's file. The commander who'd led raids into Loyalist facilities, going back for any wounded crew members. This was a man who would take great care of his needs—everything would be okay.

If he survived the next little while.

"Rules?" He wasn't going to like this.

Faolan smirked. "You seemed so fond of them when we first met. I thought you might enjoy a few of them now. Make sure you don't slip up. I'd hate to have to punish you."

Shit.

"First thing for you to realize is that until further notice, I own your cock. Got it? I get to decide when you touch it, and I most definitely get to choose if you come tonight or not."

He couldn't help but groan, knowing full well Faolan would take things to the extreme. Gar had given his word, and in his book that was a binding contract. Nodding, he slid the hand still hovering over his cock to his side while the other continued to play with his nipple. Biting his lip, he tilted his head and let his gaze wander over Faolan. The man was too perfect. He could never be Gar's, not for long at least. Good things were never his indefinitely.

He pushed the thought aside. "So, you said something about rules. Care to enlighten me?"

Faolan reached out, sliding his fingers along the inside of Gar's thigh. "Oh, I have an entire rule book I've made up for you. I've mentioned the first one."

"I can't come until you say?"

"Nope."

Gar frowned. "I have to do what you want?"

Faolan nodded. "That's correct. Rule number *two* is you can't come until I say. Make sure you don't get them confused. There's a test."

"Bastard."

"Stop touching yourself."

He let his hand fall to his side. The damage had already been done. His cock was hard and straining in his pants as his balls ached from their fullness. He wasn't good at games like this. It was part of the reason he'd lost in the shower. Stamina was one thing, but asking him to take orders and obey, much more challenging.

Faolan didn't seem to have the same problems. "Fuck, you're losing it already. Aren't you?"

Gar tried to turn his head, but Faolan's hand was on his jaw, preventing him before he realized it.

"I asked you a question. Rule number three: you have to truthfully answer me when I ask you something."

"You're making this up as you go along."

Faolan grinned. "I'm allowed. Now answer."

"Yes, Gods *damn it*! I'm about ready to come in my pants. Again."

Faolan's breath caught for a moment before he let out a sigh. "Good. Thank you. Now I want you to stand up and take those pants off. Don't want to be accused of ruining another pair. Then I want you to lie on your back, hands above your head and feet spread wide."

Gar didn't hesitate, his body and restraint too far gone to balk against the command. He jumped to his feet and worked the opening of his pants, doing his best to ignore how badly his hands shook. The cool air was a shock on his heated cock, making him want to moan from the sudden contrast. Faolan didn't move when he let go of his pants and the fabric fell down. Only once Gar climbed back on the bed did Faolan roll to his side, making space for Gar to stretch out.

It felt odd being in his bed with someone else. This was different from the previous day when Faolan had fallen dead asleep. That was almost comforting in its domesticity. No, this was alien territory. Awkwardly, he adjusted his body so he was stretched out on the mattress, faltering when he didn't quite know what to do with his hands.

"Like this." Faolan grabbed his wrists and lifted them to the black headboard. "One on top of the other. Keep them still and I promise it will be fine."

He recognized his black tie the second he saw it pulled free from beneath his pillow. Clearly, Faolan had been busy while he'd been putting the escape pod and ship into position. Faolan moved slowly, giving him ample time to shift his hands, roll away, *anything* to prevent Faolan from binding his wrists together. The silk was cool as it was looped over, under, around, and through, holding him secure. His gaze was drawn to the stark contrast of the black silk against his pale skin. If their roles were reversed, he would have found the image the most erotic thing in his recent memory. Faolan didn't stop there. Taking the remaining tail of the tie, he wound his hand around the fabric, holding it like a lead.

Only once in his life had Gar been held captive. The lack of freedom had terrified him more than the threat of death. He'd been a child then, alone and scared in a world he barely understood. He'd just witnessed the murder of his father and the abduction and murder of his sister. The sensations were beginning to feel strangely like then, sending his blood pounding through his body in desperate pulses. His chest tightened as the air refused to take purchase in his lungs.

Faolan cooed in his ear, "Gar? It's okay. Nice deep breaths."

Head falling away from Faolan, he squeezed his eyes shut and tried to calm his racing mind. This wasn't Zeten and he wasn't fourteen years old. Faolan wasn't going to try to kill him or sell him off to the sex trade. This was his ship and his bed and he could leave anytime he wanted.

"Gar?" Faolan's fingers were warm and gentle on his face. They didn't pull him, simply caressed and soothed. "Want me to stop?"

"No," he managed after a moment, his voice a harsh whisper.

"If you do at any time, I want you to tell me. Okay?"

He nodded once.

"Promise?"

He nodded again.

"No, I need you to say it."

"Promise."

Faolan pressed a kiss to his cheek. "Good boy. I think you're going to enjoy what I have in mind anyway."

Gar turned his head back, only to smile at the cocky grin on Faolan's face. "Sure about that, are you?"

"I'm nothing if not proficient in bed. Trust me."

As simple as that, he did. "What do you want me to do?"

Faolan tugged lightly on the tie, suspending Gar's hands off the mattress. "Nothing. I'm going to be in control of things and you are just going to relax your ass and enjoy it. Understand?"

"Faolan—"

"Yes or no answers only. Rule number four."

Gar ground his teeth before remembering his promise. Clearing his mind, he concentrated on letting the muscles in his back and neck loosen. It took time, but finally the tension bled away, leaving him with a dull ache. The whole while, Faolan lay patiently beside him, never once forcing an answer.

"Yes," Gar said softly.

"Good." He was rewarded with a kiss to his cheek. "Now I want you to close your eyes. No matter what happens, you're not allowed to open them or move from this position. Understand?"

He wanted to say something else, ask one of the twenty questions racing through his head. Instead, he looked over into Faolan's eyes and smiled. "Yes."

Nothing happened until he closed his eyes, this time until he was told otherwise. Once he settled, Faolan shifted so every inch of his body pressed against Gar's. Heat seeped into his skin, firing his senses and sending a ripple of energy through him. Faolan's hot breath washed over his cheek as he pressed his mouth to Gar's ear.

"I wish you could see yourself like this, all spread out and waiting for me. Your cock is so red and hard, gods, that must hurt."

Gar moaned, bucking his hips into the air. Faolan made a tsking sound in the back of his throat and bit down on Gar's earlobe.

"I said no moving."

Gar settled back, shocked at the intensity of the sensations. He jackknifed upward when Faolan latched on to the sensitive patch of skin below his ear, sucking hard. Fingers squeezed tight against the binding of the tie, all he could do was hold on and give himself over to the onslaught.

He scraped teeth along Gar's shoulder, nipping at the skin around his nipple. Faolan sucked the swollen peak into his mouth, not stopping until Gar choked back a sob. While it was completely arousing, Gar could also feel the care and affection in every touch. It was overwhelming.

"Too much?" Faolan asked, his mouth wet against Gar's chest as he moved lower. "Because I'm about to let go of the tie and I don't want you to move. If you don't think you can handle it, then I'll have to skip what I was planning."

"No."

Gar didn't need to be told part of the plan was Faolan sucking his cock. It was obvious from the trail of open-mouthed kisses Faolan was marking him with. He tried to keep still, not wanting to jeopardize the night's outcome, still shocked by the underlying emotion. Faolan bit firmly into his side, making him gasp with the slight pain of teeth and stubble on sensitive flesh.

"Good." Faolan licked the wounded area. "I'm letting go now."

Placing the tail of the tie in the center of Gar's chest, Faolan caged Gar's ribs with his hands, flexing his fingers into the skin.

"It's been a very long time since I've been with a man as fit as you." Faolan circled Gar's navel with his tongue. "Young, handsome. Nice, thick cock. You have no idea how much I enjoyed having you fuck me the other day."

Hot breath tickled the tip of Gar's shaft as Faolan positioned himself between Gar's legs. A powerful shudder rolled through his body, and he had to fight the urge to reach down and bury his hands in Faolan's long brown hair. Gods, he wanted to see it, watch as Faolan took the tip of his cock into his mouth, cheeks hollowing from the suction.

He wasn't expecting Faolan to suckle his balls.

"Gods!"

The pirate's wicked tongue swirled around the sac until Gar's arousal rocketed to the near-bursting point. Unable to keep the noises inside any longer, Gar let his mouth fall open, freeing the moans and gasps Faolan's touch elicited.

"Oh, that's it. I want to hear you. Let me know how much you like it."

He didn't hold back. Thrashing his head on the pillow, he cried out as Faolan lifted his legs over his shoulders, opening his body wide. The first touch of Faolan's tongue against his opening made him gasp. Faolan teased the ring of muscles with broad swipes, each one sloppy and wet. Faolan soaked Gar's hole until he could feel saliva dripping down his ass cheeks. He didn't think it could get more intense, until Faolan tightened his tongue and drove the tip into his ass.

"Fuck!"

Faolan hummed his agreement and continued to fuck his face into Gar until he couldn't think, couldn't breathe from the pleasure. Gods, Faolan hadn't even touched his cock and he was about ready to come. His thighs shook from the tension, and he squeezed Faolan's head. With one final swipe, Faolan lifted his head to wipe his mouth on Gar's inner thigh.

"Like that?" Faolan's voice was nothing more than a harsh whisper.

"Yes." He didn't care that he sounded needy. He wanted Faolan to do something. Anything. He needed to keep this connection alive with Faolan almost as much as he needed to come. "Please."

He heard Faolan's breath hitch, but refused to go against his wishes and open his eyes. Instead he did his best to calm his racing heart and overcharged arousal.

"Open your eyes."

Gar did, immediately seeking Faolan out. The sight was one he wouldn't soon forget. Faolan's brown hair was plastered to the side of his face with sweat and spit. Cheeks flushed, his eyes were heavy with lust and focused on Gar. His lips were wet and swollen, inviting and most certainly fuckable.

"Say it again. I want to see you when you ask nicely."

Gar wasn't sure what Faolan meant at first, until he remembered what the pirate had said that first night in the alley. Gar knew it was a type of surrender, one step closer to a place he'd never gone with another person. Swallowing, he realized Faolan was the only one who he'd ever consider giving himself over to. "*Please.*"

Faolan's eyes rolled back into his head, and he groaned. "I can't wait anymore. I need you."

Gar wasn't sure if he was ready for this, but if any man was going to fuck him, he knew he wanted it to be Faolan. Heart racing, Gar gripped the ties binding his wrists and spread his legs a bit farther. He could do this, could trust Faolan to make it good for him, even if it pushed him to the edge of his comfort zone.

So he was shocked when Faolan lowered his head and sucked his cock, wetting it thoroughly, only to pull back before he could properly enjoy the sensations. Even more confusing was when Faolan reached for the lube, squeezed a generous amount, and coated Gar's cock with it.

"What are you—"

Faolan silenced him by crushing his mouth to Gar's. The kiss wasn't neat or even particularly skillful. It was passionate and imprecise, perfect in every way. Faolan shifted their bodies, straddling Gar's hips with his thighs and reaching back to line up Gar's cock with his ass.

"I know what you were thinking, but that's not something I would take from you. You need to give it to me willingly." Faolan's moans filled the bedroom as he let his body sink down.

Gar reached his bound hands for Faolan's neck, but they were quickly shoved back down. Faolan captured Gar's wrists in one hand and pressed them into the mattress.

"I said keep those there."

Gar bucked up his hips. "Want to touch you."

Faolan lifted his body at the same time, preventing Gar from getting any further penetration. "This isn't about what you want. Now shut up and enjoy yourself."

Muscles squeezed as he lowered himself to Gar's lap. The closeness was almost too much for Gar to take. It was overwhelming, yet he wanted so much more from Faolan.

Faolan didn't wait for his body to adjust, instead fucking himself down on Gar in short, steady pulses. Gar knew there must be a small degree of discomfort for him, but Faolan didn't seem to mind. Faolan visibly fought to keep his eyes open and his gaze locked on Gar's face, but it was easy to see his struggle was a losing one.

"So tight," Gar said, this time successful in fucking up into Faolan. "Your ass is perfect."

"So . . . big." Faolan threw his head back as he slammed his body down.

The spike of pleasure nearly took Gar over the edge. He snapped his mouth shut and tightened the muscles in his legs, praying it was enough to hold himself back.

"Don't you dare come," Faolan panted out in between thrusts. "Not until I say so. Me first this time."

Gar tried to think up as many disgusting images as he could, hoping the imagery would help stave off his release, but everything that came to mind quickly morphed into an erotic landscape. He wasn't going to last much longer—he needed to beat Faolan at his own game.

He turned his face and licked the inside of Faolan's forearm. "You're so tight around my cock. You haven't let many people fuck you. Have you?"

Faolan growled, his grip tightening on Gar's wrists. "Don't."

Gar grinned. "You love it though. Gods, your cock is leaking you're so turned on."

Faolan dropped his chin to his chest. "Shut . . . up. Yes or no *only*."

You want to play it that way, eh? "Yes, yes, yes." He started the steady chant soft, keeping it in time with the rise and fall of Faolan's body.

Eyes open, he saw the moment Faolan realized what he was doing. Faolan shook his head and chuckled before locking his gaze on Gar's. The next yes died in Gar's mouth as he lost himself in what he saw reflected back at him. Emotions he wasn't used to seeing directed at him filled Faolan's eyes—genuine amusement, lust, and something that looked like adoration. His chest tightened, and his stomach flipped. He didn't deserve this.

The moment fled once Faolan's eyes rolled back into his head as Gar snapped his hips up sharply. Faolan cried out when Gar repeated the action, knowing he'd hit the other man's prostate.

"Again," Faolan begged.

"Yes, gods yes."

Faolan clenched around Gar's cock, every muscle in his body tightening for a moment before a sudden scream erupted from him. Cum shot out from his shaft, covering Gar's stomach and chest with thick, white ropes. Faolan didn't stop slamming his body down, riding out his orgasm until he was left gasping for air and sweat covered every inch of his skin.

Gar managed to keep from following Faolan over bliss's edge. He held on, body poised on the brink, but waiting for the command to fall. Faolan slowed his pace but didn't stop. He leaned over Gar, cum now binding their chests together, and kissed him hard. Tongues caressed until they were both left gasping for air. Faolan finally lifted his head, but didn't pull away too far. Their lips still touched as Faolan smiled.

"Fuck me till you come."

Gar looped his hands around Faolan's neck. With a practiced flip, he rolled them over until he was on top, allowing him the leverage needed to piston into Faolan's welcoming body. It was only a matter of seconds before his orgasm won out, dragging a cry from his chest and cum from his body.

Neither man spoke, instead communicating through a series of kisses and sighs. Gar nuzzled Faolan's neck until the skin was red from his stubble.

"You love making rules, but can't seem to follow them very well," Faolan said, slapping Gar's ass. "I should punish you for that."

His rules had kept him safe until now. Faolan had changed things.

"Rules are meant to be broken." He rolled onto his side and held his hands up. "Do you mind?"

Faolan made short work of the bindings, winding the tie around his hand once it was free of Gar. Holding it to his nose, Faolan breathed in deep. "I'm keeping this."

Gar stretched out beside him, massaging his wrists as the blood flow returned. "Loot to add to your booty, Captain?"

When Faolan didn't laugh or come back with a witty retort, Gar turned to look at him. "Faolan?"

The long frown on Faolan's face was an unfamiliar sight. He kept his gaze away from Gar, making it difficult to get a sense of what was going on in his head. Reaching out, Gar traced a finger down the length of Faolan's neck. "You okay?"

"Despite what you think," Faolan said, his voice hesitant, "I don't normally do this sort of thing."

"Have sex? Do I need to remind you of the circumstances of our meeting?"

"I'm serious, Gar." Faolan finally turned his face to look at him. "I don't do this."

Walking over the edge of a cliff felt remarkably similar. "Talk? Cuddle? Help me out here."

Faolan's lips compressed and his jaw clenched, but he said nothing. The urge to punch something, or *someone*, reared up inside Gar. Gods, this was the benefit of staying alone in his ship in the middle of space. Things were nice and clear, with no cocky, infuriating space pirates to piss him off. He knew it was too good to be true—too good for him to have any part of it.

"Look, sorry if I'm coming across like an idiot here, but I'm a tad confused." He pressed the heels of his hands to his eyes. "You said you don't do *this* with no indication of what *this* is. Do you want to do *this* with me or do you want to run screaming out the airlock? I know my preference is quickly shifting to the latter."

The dip and pull of the mattress caught his attention. He lifted his hands from his face and stared. "Where are you going?"

"You need to rest. I'm going to go program the ship to take us to the *Belle Kurve*." Faolan paused halfway through buttoning up his pants to face Gar. "Unless you have a problem with that? It's your ship after all, and I wouldn't want to piss you off."

Things had soured between them, and for the life of him, Gar didn't have a clue what he'd done wrong. "Not at all. Just don't ding her coming out of orbit."

Faolan nodded. "Get some rest. You've been up for a while now. I'll wake you when we get close."

"Thanks." Faolan was out the door before the word left Gar's lips.

Rolling onto his back, he let his forearm fall across his face and let out a sigh. *What the fuck just happened?*

CHAPTER

TEN

The cool air of the cockpit did little to sooth Faolan's annoyance. He first thought Gar would follow him to push matters, grind him down until a confession fell from his mouth. He should have realized Gar didn't need to sink to such tactics, especially when his mark had such a big mouth and a normal willingness to talk.

Well, not this time.

Somehow, over the hour he had Gar tied and bound, naked and wanting on his bed, his emotions had crept out to play. How they'd escaped his notice, he still wasn't sure, but there they stood: bright and colorful, inevitable and messy. In their short time together, Gar had accomplished what only one other person had managed over the course of his life—he made Faolan want to love.

The ship's computer beeped softly at him, feeding a steady stream of readings from the sector. The noise was soothing, though it did little to clear his mind. It didn't make sense, his feelings for this man. He was eight years Gar's senior and a criminal living on the edge of proper society, hunted on a daily basis by others. He had nothing to offer Gar that Gar didn't already possess on his own. Faolan's life was his ship and his crew. They looked to him to keep them safe and provide for their livelihood—the very things he knew Gar instinctively avoided.

Faolan couldn't escape his obligations—never really wanted to.

Since Kayla's death—gods, had it *really* been ten years—he'd made a point of not attaching himself romantically to anyone. With his illness and impending death, he didn't want to put someone else through the emotional pain of dealing with him through the end stages. It was bad enough he knew Mace would stick by his side until the bitter end, even if it was the last thing he wanted to put her through. He really hoped she didn't find out.

If he were being honest with himself—and he tried to do that if nothing else—if there was one person he could choose to be there with him, it would be Gar. Yes, it was selfish and totally out of character from the flamboyant Captain Wolf everyone was used to seeing, but he was only a man. A lonely one at that. There was something about the bounty hunter—a solid core of unshakable strength he would be able to draw on to help him focus.

He wouldn't do it. He didn't want to put that on Gar.

Closing his eyes, he rested his head back on the pilot's chair and did his best to ignore the overwhelming scent of Gar in the room. Despite all their differences, their love of space was at least the same. He recognized the look of awe when Gar stared out into the vastness of the space before them. Most men and women who lived amongst the stars shared it—the realization that you were nothing more than a speck in the enormity of the universe. It was a humbling thought.

The steady beeping of the computer woke him from his doze. Shit, he'd fallen asleep again. The alarm indicated new ships had entered the sector—com beacons announcing them as belonging to the guild. He pushed every thought he could from his mind and watched as a battery of vessels moved to the battle's location and scanned the drifting hulks of the ships. He knew the *Geilt* was safe from their sensors, but he wanted to be prepared to pull out of orbit if necessary.

The rescue operation of Krieg's ships took longer than Faolan had anticipated. According to the com chatter, the explosions had not only rendered the surviving people blind, but taken out all shields, leaving them open to damage from floating debris. Two of the five ships were unreachable and the crews were presumed dead. The recovery was quickly followed by a trace of their radiation trail, which nicely led the guild ships back to the path of the escape pod and the end stop of the dimension gate.

"Come on, boys, figure out where we've gone."

Krieg clearly needed to hire more highly skilled staff. Or at the very least, stop trying to kill off his top operatives. It took at least another hour for Krieg's team to crack the dimension gate locator relay and the destination of the last object. Thankfully, this was a little-used sector of space and no other ships had passed through since Gar sent the pod on its way. They finally activated the gate and space folded around them, swallowing the ships whole.

He let out the breath he'd been holding and pressed his forehead to the computer console. Another disaster averted. A grand total of twelve hours and twenty minutes from the time Gar had sent the escape pod out until Krieg's goons left to chase the bait. He needed to move them quickly now to escape the guild operatives' notice.

Easing the ship higher into orbit, he set their destination and pushed it to full throttle. The *Geilt* was a small but maneuverable ship, but what he hadn't realized was how sensitive it was to the pilot's commands. It took him a few minutes to get a feel for her. A grin split his face once he got the control he wanted. Gar flew the ship in such a way Faolan had never realized the full extent of Gar's skills. Impressive.

The internal com system beeped at him. "We're moving."

Gar's voice was thick and sleep-heavy. Images of his naked body stretched out beneath white sheets blossomed in the forefront of Faolan's mind. His cock twitched its appreciation at the thought and seemed more than willing to follow through. Too bad his brain had entered into the equation. Reaching down with one hand to squeeze his uncooperative shaft, he hit the com button with the other.

"Krieg's team has finally left. You didn't tell me you were the only intelligent one in the bunch."

"How long did it take them to crack the gate?"

"An hour ten."

"Gods. I'm glad he fired me. Bunch of idiots."

Faolan chuckled. "Is that what you're telling yourself now? He *fired* you?"

"Shut up, Wolf." There was a long pause as bed sheets were shifted. "I'm getting dressed and will be up there soon."

"Don't bother. I need to get us in position before we can jump and meet up with my ship. Enjoy the lie in."

"Faolan—"

"Oh, for the gods' sake, Stitt. Rest! It's not like you're going to get a lot more of it over the next few weeks. Krieg has a long reach."

Another pause, only this time there was no sound to give Faolan any indication of what was going on. He knew Gar would be debating the *right* thing to do versus what he *should* do in his mind. The thought of Gar's scowl made him smirk.

"I thought we had established you trusted me to drive your ship, Stitt?"

"Are you sure you're fine up there?"

The question caught him off guard. He straightened in the chair, fists balled at his side. "I'm better than you are. Plus I need to contact my ship. Don't want you getting any information on my communication codes."

He could practically hear Gar's eye roll. "Fine. Wreck the *Geilt* and I'll kill you on the spot."

"You say the sweetest things."

He slammed his hand down on the com button to end the conversation. *Stupid, childish ass!* Why did he think he'd felt anything at all for Gar? He would never trust him, let him beneath the solid armor he wore to protect his emotions. Faolan learned long ago he couldn't do anything less than hand his heart over to his partner, no matter how painful the process would be. He refused to be a part of any one-sided relationship.

He froze, hand suspended over the ship's controls. Sure, acknowledging he had the beginning of feelings for Gar was one thing, but a relationship? He'd only bloody well known the man for a few days! Had he not sat here a short time ago saying he didn't want a relationship? He didn't, did he?

Fuck.

Work—he needed to get back to the task at hand. Get back to his ship, get the stone, sell it, and pay his crew. Then he'd see if there was enough left to pay for his medication and allow him to disappear off into a little-known sector of this galaxy to die in peace.

Far away from Gar Stitt.

Punching in the jump coordinates, he gave half a thought to contacting Gar to prepare him. Instead, he hit the ship warning alarm, slid the *Geilt* where it needed to be in front of the gate, pressed the button, and held on for dear life.

The dimension shift was worse than before. His stomach bottomed out as they shot back into normal space, and his head spun madly. A line of sweat formed on his upper lip, one he wiped away with the back of his hand. He needed to keep it together a little bit longer before he could allow himself to fall apart. Not until he was locked safely in his quarters.

This was a heavily traveled sector, and he needed to move the ship a safe distance away from the gate to prevent a collision. It proved more challenging than he first anticipated, the spinning of his head refusing to go away. Rocking the ship more than he liked, he finally managed to get her safely off the main traffic route. The increased communication lines in the sector made it easy for him to piggyback a signal off three relays to reach his desired target.

"*Belle Kurve*, come in. Daddy's come home with the booty."

Galactic static crackled to life on the vid screen as his message traveled gods knew where. He hit the repeater button, sending it out into the cosmos once again. Concern grew in his chest, but was quickly squashed when a high-pitched whine filled the cabin as the *Kurve*'s jacked frequency cut through.

"You asshole!" Mace's smiling face popped up on the screen after a brief wait. Faolan laughed and pressed his fingertip to the image of her nose. "You had us worried sick, Faolan."

"Sorry, pet, but the hunter and I ran into a little bit of difficulty."

Mace crossed her arms across her chest and glared at him. "What trouble? Am I going to have to string this jerk up or did you skin him alive already?"

"Not at all. My captor was double-crossed and stabbed in the back for good measure by Krieg. Might want to consider giving the poor ex-hunter a hug instead." He winked.

"Pardon? Hug?" Mace leaned forward, eyes fixed on his. "Do you have a thing for this boy?"

Little wench was too perceptive for her own good. "I assure you, Stitt and I share a purely professional relationship."

She cocked an eyebrow at him. "Did he use his cuffs on you?"

Grinning, he winked again. "Hell yes. But I got to use a tie on him."

Mace laughed. "You are something else, Wolf. I swear you could flirt yourself out of a death squad."

The way she'd said his name sent a tingle crawling down his spine. It was no different than the thousand other times his name had slipped from her lips, only this time it had changed, grown oddly familiar.

Mace frowned. "What? You look like you swallowed a *tar drake*."

"Nothing." He waved her away with his hand. "You ready to bring me to my baby?"

"Just waiting on word from you."

"Good girl. Let's hit meeting point beta in five hours. Come in hot and we'll jump out together."

"You got it, boss. You good until then? Anything you want me to have ready for you when you get here?"

"Hydro vodka. A big, chilled bottle of hydro vodka would be amazing."

Mace tugged on her earlobe and grinned. "You bringing your hunter on board or are we leaving him behind?"

A good question—one he didn't have an answer to yet. "I'll keep you posted. Be ready in either case."

"Just keep him in line if you do. You know how I feel about them."

"They are the scum of the universe and must be burned out of existence. Yes, I'm well aware." It wasn't as if he'd forgotten the life he'd rescued Mace from all those years ago. "I promise you'll like Stitt. He's bitchy like you."

Mace flipped him the finger.

He laughed. "See you soon, pet. Wolf out."

The screen winked out as the cockpit door slid open. Gar stood in the entrance, dressed in a full black suit, including a vest and a blood-red tie. The image he painted should have been slightly ridiculous, but it wasn't. Gar looked more at ease in his formal wear than most men Faolan had met over the years. The sexy cut of the fabric certainly flattered his athletic frame. He looked older than his twenty-four years, a beacon shining amidst the chaos, a rock that Faolan desperately wanted to cling to.

Gods, no wonder he was starting to fall for the man.

"Is everything all right up here?" Gar didn't come any closer. His hands twitched nervously at his sides.

Faolan hated that he'd turned the otherwise confident bounty hunter into an uncertain schoolboy. Normally he'd make some quick, offhand remark or shoot him a leer and all would be right between them. Really, it should be simple. But as he opened his mouth to say something, he found himself unable to brush things off.

"Faolan?"

It wasn't fair to either of them to go down this road, but despite all arguments to the contrary, he couldn't stop himself. Rising to his feet, he walked over to Gar. He loved how tall the other man was, that he didn't have to bend over to accommodate for a height difference. It also meant he couldn't hide from Gar's questioning gaze. Faolan unbuttoned the suit jacket, leaving the vest alone, and toyed with the edge of the material. He kept focused on the jacket and how his fingertip teased the buttonhole.

"I made contact with my ship. Set the rendezvous for five hours from now."

Gar reached up and brushed a finger alongside Faolan's. "Location?"

"I'll program the path soon. Then you can drop me off and head out if you want."

Gar's hand stilled. "Is that what you want?"

"I meant what I said earlier about setting you up with some of my contacts, but if you want to strike out on your own, then I won't hold you back."

"The stone? What are you planning to do with it now?"

Yes, the damn stone. "I still have two options. I can try to broker a deal with Krieg—although I'll need to be extra cautious—or put out some additional feelers and see if anyone else bites. I won't get the asking price I was hoping for, but there are lots of rich egotists in the universe."

"That could take some time."

Something Faolan didn't have a lot of. "It doesn't matter. I need to make a killing off this thing."

"Debts to pay?" Gar covered Faolan's hand with his own, pale skin shining against Faolan's natural tan. "There are easier and less dangerous ways to make money."

"I can always turn myself in for the bounty. I hear I'm worth two million credits now."

"Are you going to ignore me from now on?"

Faolan snapped his gaze up. "Thought we were talking here. How is that ignoring you?"

Gar rolled his eyes before reaching up to thread his fingers through Faolan's hair. Faolan winced when he brushed over a large bump from the beating he'd taken. Gar closed his eyes, a pained look on his face.

"No wonder you don't want me around. I'm a complete bastard."

Shit. "It's not that—"

"I beat you unconscious, then got you in my bed. We have the most amazing sex I've ever had *in my life*, only to have you tell me that you don't do *this* and run away." Gar closed his eyes and took a breath. "To make matters worse, my boss stabbed us both in the back, nearly blowing us out of space. If that isn't reason enough to hate me . . ."

Faolan had wanted to see the man beneath the mask, and for the first time he was getting a true glimpse. It wasn't what he'd hoped to find—Gar was broken. Cupping Gar's face in his hands, he stepped in and captured his mouth in a gentle kiss. This wasn't like anything they'd shared in the past—slow, tentative, and tasting a bit like forgiveness. His body shook from the intensity of the unspoken words passing between them.

I didn't mean it.

I have nothing to offer.

I'm so alone and you're the only one who can save me.

Don't go.

They pulled apart at the same time, pressing their foreheads together. Faolan didn't do relationships, not any longer. He was wanted for more crimes than he cared to recount. Most of them were even legitimate claims. His intentions or even the end results were irrelevant. He was a criminal with no hope to offer anyone a stable life. It wasn't something he wanted for himself, even if the consequences left him alone.

But with Gar there was the potential for something. Gar understood what this life was like, the solitude. While they would never have a traditional relationship, Faolan could at least take advantage of Gar's embrace while he could still lift his arms . . . and end it before Gar found out how ill he really was.

"Come back to my ship. We can tether the *Geilt* to her so you don't need to worry about leaving her behind."

Gar tightened his grip on Faolan's waist. "I'm not good with crowds."

"A ship with twenty people, all wanted for various crimes in case you're curious, is hardly a crowd." Gar tried to pull back, but Faolan didn't let him go. "Come with me. Just for a bit. You can head out to the middle of nowhere after you've had a rest."

"I doubt I'll be high on anyone's list of people to see. I've made a living out of catching and killing people like you."

"There isn't anyone like me, Stitt." He placed a kiss on the tip of Gar's nose before finally letting him go. "If nothing else, come get a look at the stone. Maybe we can figure out why Krieg wanted us dead so badly."

Gar stiffened. "I don't need to know the reason. It's not going to change the fact I plan to rip him apart."

"Of course you need to know the reason." He couldn't believe the normally restrained man would even consider doing something without thinking the consequences through. "If this is something bigger than the man himself, we need to be prepared. Deal with it properly so things can't come back to haunt us."

Gar slapped his hand against the side of his leg. "You think you can actually discover the truth?"

"If I can't, then at the very least I know people who can."

Shifting to shove his hands into his pants pockets, Gar shrugged. "What about this *thing* you don't do?"

"We don't do it. Doesn't mean we can't do something else." A wave of dizziness hit him, forcing him to reach out and grab the pilot's seat for support. At the last moment, he managed to spin the chair around and fall into it, making the move look intended. When Gar didn't react, Faolan grinned and hoped the con would last a bit longer. "Either way we need to get my ship. It gives you five hours to make up your mind. Consider the invitation open and an opportunity to restock the pitiful storage cupboards you have back there."

Gar snorted. "Let it go, Wolf."

"You'll die of starvation in the middle of space with no one to find you. I think my plan is the better option."

"I *do* have a food replicator."

"I've shared my opinion of that thing. Real food is necessary."

"Gods, this is going to be a long five hours."

Faolan laughed and shifted over to the copilot seat when Gar nudged his leg. "It's all a matter of perspective, Stitt. I plan on fully enjoying myself the entire time."

"Shut up and plug the coordinates into the nav system so we can get there sometime this century."

Faolan chuckled as he leaned in and did just that. His head was still funny, and he didn't dare push his luck any further. The sooner he could get back to the *Belle Kurve*, the better it would be for all of them.

"Coordinates in and locked. Ready for blastoff, Captain."

Gar rolled his eyes. "You're a child. You know that, right?"

"You act as if you're one foot from the grave. If you can't enjoy the time you have in this universe, then what's the point in being here?"

Their conversation drifted from banter to piloting speak as they navigated through the crowded sector. It really was the last place anyone would suspect to find a man with a bounty the size of his. The lanes were filled with Loyalist ships and outlander colonist convoys heading to their various planets. Any one of the people out there would jump at the chance to turn him in, dead or alive, and here he was, safe and sound in the belly of a bounty hunter's ship.

Ah, the irony.

Gar slipped through a security grid using a code designed to mimic a Loyalist security cruiser. Faolan would have to get his hands on that little gem before Gar left him all alone. His heart clenched a little at the thought, but he knew it really was for the best. The silence between them fell away as Gar twisted in his seat to stare at him.

"Faolan?"

"Yup."

"If that offer stands, I think I'd like to see your ship." Gar shifted in his seat, smoothing down the front of his suit. "It would do me some good to practice my people skills."

Faolan really shouldn't have been grinning, but he couldn't help it. "Good. I'm glad."

"Good."

"You don't actually *have* any people skills. Just so you know."

Gar sighed. "Thanks for that."

"Anytime."

The computer beeped again, indicating they were coming out of the main traffic lane and heading into the back quadrant of the sector.

"Faolan?"

"Hmm?"

"I . . . don't do *this* either."

He turned his head so he could see the blush covering Gar's face. "Good to know."

Very good indeed.

CHAPTER
ELEVEN

The *Belle Kurve* was bigger than Gar had expected. In his experience, space pirates and con men liked to keep as low a profile as possible. Of course, Faolan was in a category all his own.

"I can't believe that beast is yours."

"What's wrong with her?" The note of offended pride was clear in Faolan's voice. "She's one of the best things to ever happen to me."

"Want me to leave the two of you alone?"

"How old are you again?" Faolan asked, glaring.

Amusement warmed Gar's insides, and it was a struggle not to let it show. The longer he spent in Faolan's company, the more he found he enjoyed the things around him. It wasn't right, but even he wasn't strong enough to fight against the colossal force of Faolan's good nature.

Typing a code into the com system, Faolan leaned back and kicked his feet up. "I just gave them the all clear. Now we just need to sit back and relax."

What the hell? "You're kidding."

"Watch and learn, young one."

The proximity sensors began to wail in warning as the *Belle Kurve* moved dangerously close to the *Geilt*'s hull. Normally, he would have adjusted his trajectory to avoid a collision, but he held still in his seat. Barely.

"They *do* know you're on board, right?"

Faolan cocked an eyebrow. "Concerned?"

"Just for my sanity. I hope your pilot is as good as you think he is." The larger ship dwarfed the *Geilt* as it hovered along the top of the hull. Then nothing. Gar leaned forward to peer out the window. "This is all rather anticlimactic."

"Might want to sit your gorgeous ass down. Don't want you getting hurt."

He managed to reclaim his seat as a bright blue shield encased both ships. He opened his mouth to object when he was thrown back in his chair. A pocket of space opened around them only to spit them out a minute later. Gaping, he turned to look at Faolan.

"You have a jump drive on your ship? No wonder the authorities can't catch you."

Faolan didn't answer. His eyes were squeezed shut and a strand of his hair was plastered to his cheek with sweat.

"You okay?" Gar brushed the hair away, tucking it behind Faolan's ear. "You're burning up."

"Just a little spacesick." Faolan smiled, but didn't open his eyes. "Give me a minute and I'll be right as a Terrin wind during the dry season."

"I've been in space for most of the past six years, and I've never met anyone who gets spacesick because of a dimension jump."

"Well, now you have. Hardly anything really." Taking a deep breath, Faolan wiped his hand across his mouth, sat up, and grinned. "See, I'm feeling better already. Now how about we get your ship linked up so I can get my sorry ass back home?"

Gar knew it wasn't as simple as Faolan wanted him to believe. If he'd learned nothing else over the past few days, he knew Captain Wolf might come across as an open and honest crook, but the man hid everything behind his wide smile and easy nature. Clearly not wanting to discuss it further, Faolan took over the com system.

"Ricco! Are you the psycho flying my baby?"

The blue-hued face of an older Terrin came to view. "Boss. You brought us a present?"

"Nope, the *Geilt* is off-limits. Hear me? Make sure to pass that along to everyone else. Captain's orders."

"Yes, sir."

"Lower the clamps. We're going to tether her so Stitt and I can come on board."

Ricco grunted. "Bounty hunters."

"Hey now, be nice. This particular bounty hunter saved my ass."

"Of course, Captain." Ricco was clearly not impressed.

The screen blinked off, and Gar wanted to groan. "Pleasant fellow."

"His brother sold him out to one of your kind a few years back. Let's just say your chosen profession isn't high on his list of favorites. You'll find that's the same for a lot of my crew."

"I'm not thrilled with the idea of having my ship locked to a pirate's, but you don't see me complaining."

"Gods, no, you never would." Faolan stood, placing a hand on Gar's shoulder. "Let me show you how the other half lives."

Gar was surprised when Faolan didn't remove his hand, only shifted to press it against his lower back. The firm support was a comfort when it shouldn't have been, sending a pleasant hum through his body. Just as surprising was the urge to reciprocate the touch. He'd never been one to seek out physical comfort, unlike Faolan who appeared to thrive on it.

"You'll love the crew, but don't be offended if they aren't too welcoming at first. I'm completely confident your warm charm and quick wit will win them over in no time."

"Right." He wasn't about to take it for granted Faolan's crew would be as open-minded as Faolan was. He'd dressed with his blades, including the ankle knife he rarely used. Sure, they would be easily detectable if someone searched him, but he didn't intend for anyone to get close enough to check.

If Faolan was half as intelligent as Gar took him to be, he already knew Gar was well armed. It was somewhat comforting to know he wouldn't be asked to remove them before going on board. At the very least he hoped Faolan wouldn't prove him wrong and try to make a show of it, publicly disarming him to set the tone. He'd kick his ass if he did.

The airlock for the upper hull was located in the main cabin of the ship. It was a containment area that provided Gar a buffer against pirates if he were ever attacked and boarded. He did his best to ignore the feeling of discomfort and unease as he activated the ladder and climbed up to release the hatch.

"As much as I love the view from your behind, better let me go first." Faolan spanked Gar's ass cheek. He'd retrieved his remaining clothing from the main cabin, but hadn't yet fully dressed the part of space pirate. "They're just as likely to shoot you between the eyes as they are to offer you a drink. I'll soften them up first."

Despite Faolan's levity, Gar knew better than to argue. Pressing the security code, he waited until the hydraulics released before jumping down. He bowed deep at the waist, allowing Faolan to move past. "Sir."

Faolan grinned as he pulled his green jacket on and fastened the belt holding his sword. "Charming. You have no idea how well you're going to fit in, Stitt."

"Very reassuring."

He couldn't help his gaze as it drifted to Faolan's ass, watching the play of muscles as he moved up the rungs.

"I can feel you staring."

Gar fought his smile. "Just making sure you don't break anything."

Faolan banged on the hatch three times, waited a moment before banging twice more. Only then did he throw the door open.

"Daddy's home, children. I brought company, so get out the clean linen."

Gar stood at the bottom of the ladder, forced to listen to the clamor and riot of voices in the ship above him. Warm greetings and sharp barks of laughter filtered down through the combined metal hulls, dragging feelings of jealous insecurity from him. He'd never had close relationships with any of the other hunters of the guild. Rarely did they communicate, and never did they work together. Too risky. No one trusted any of the others enough to complete operations without Jason's direct involvement. It hadn't helped make Gar any friends when others in the guild learned about his role as Jason's protégé and top hunter. There was always someone bucking for his position.

Why he'd thought a band of space pirates would be the same, he wasn't sure. The proof of his incorrect assumptions was currently assaulting his senses. This wasn't going to work. He couldn't shed years of protective barriers to fit into Faolan's band of thugs, no matter how badly he wanted a place to belong.

"Gar!"

The temptation to stay on his ship, have Faolan release the clamps so he could disappear, was almost too much. If it weren't for Faolan's strange reaction to the dimension jump and Gar's unexplained urge to make sure Faolan was okay, he'd do just that.

"Gar!" Faolan poked his head down through the hatch. "Get your sorry self up here. I promise no one will kill you. Today."

"So reassuring." He straightened his jacket before climbing the ladder.

The voices died completely as he pulled himself up and stood for the first time on the *Belle Kurve*. Not wanting to give any indication of his unease, he cleared his mind of all thoughts, relaxed his body, and prepared himself to jump back down the hatch if necessary.

Faolan simply shot him a broad grin. "Everyone, this is Gar Stitt. The man was sent to kill me, but quickly saw how drab the universe would be without my charm and good looks. Instead, he's stopped by to spend some time with your sorry asses."

Gar snorted on impulse. No one around him reacted in any way, giving the entire situation a menacing edge. Never one to be easily intimidated, he let his gaze sweep across the ragged collection of people, taking in faces and physical characteristics. Not the full complement of the crew, only half a dozen or so. Including Ricco, the grumpy Terrin Gar recognized from the com.

"I expect you to treat Gar with the same respect we show everyone else who comes on board." Faolan stepped over to Ricco and placed a hand on his shoulder. "I was serious when I said he saved my life. He didn't have to. Could have turned me in for the bounty or dumped my body out an airlock countless times. He's got nowhere to go now, so that makes him ours."

Time ticked on in Gar's head as he waited for the crew to pass judgment over him. Surprisingly, Ricco stepped away from Faolan to come stand mere inches from Gar's face.

"Bounty hunter?" Ricco grumbled, eyes squinted as he looked Gar over.

"For a while now."

"Zeten?"

"Yes. Terrin?"

Ricco snorted. "What gave it away?"

Gar took in the trademark blue skin and cocked an eyebrow. "Bad breath and body odor."

Snickers and chuckles filtered and spread throughout the gathering until Ricco grinned. "We can keep him."

Faolan clapped his hands together and laughed. "Excellent! I'd hate to kill him after all that time I spent teaching him how to behave."

"In your dreams, Wolf." Gar rolled his eyes and nodded to Ricco as the Terrin left the room.

"You'll meet the rest of the crew soon enough." Faolan led him toward the corridor. "We couldn't pull them all away from their stations to come worship at your brilliantly clad feet. Though I'm surprised Mace wasn't here."

Gar froze, his feet unable to take another step. "Who?"

No, it couldn't be. The name wasn't *that* uncommon in certain sectors of the galaxy. His sister was long dead—this was clearly someone else. His rationalizations didn't do anything to slow the pounding of his heart or the sick feeling in his stomach.

Faolan turned to face him, his face contorted into a mask of confusion. "Mace Simms, my second-in-command and the only other Zeten I can tolerate. Don't tell me you tried to bring Mace in on a bounty, because even I won't be able to stop the bloodshed if you did."

"Oh gods." Gar's legs threatened to give out on him. Faolan grabbed him tight around the waist and led him to a chair.

"Captain?" A young man moved up beside them.

"Get Mace," Faolan snapped. "Now!"

It *couldn't* be Mace, not *his* Mace. She was dead, murdered the same day as their father by the Loyalist sergeant sent to arrest their family. It simply wasn't plausible to even imagine she was alive— *safe*—living as a space pirate on Faolan's ship.

"Gar, look at me." Faolan kept his voice low. Leaning in so their foreheads touched, Faolan smiled softly. "That's it. I need you to tell me what's going on before she arrives."

He didn't have a clue himself. "Where did you find her?"

"Zeten, believe it or not. Last time I ever set foot on that hellhole of a planet you call home."

Gar swallowed down the rising bile. "Oh gods. It can't be her."

Faolan gave him a shake. "*Who?*"

The door whooshed open, and Gar pulled away from Faolan. A young woman bounded through, marching directly toward them.

"Faolan, you know I can't bloody well stand bounty hunters. Why the hell did you want me to . . .?"

Their eyes locked—blue met hazel, shock and surprise transferring between them. The years suddenly evaporated, and Gar was once again a terrified fourteen-year-old, crying over his sister's body in a back room of a Zeten detention camp. It had been Gar's fault the Loyalist bastards had found their family in the first place.

"No," Mace whispered.

Gar swallowed hard. "You're dead."

"Garratt?" She took a tentative step closer. "Is that you?"

Gar shook his head repeatedly. "No, no, no. They told me you were dead. They showed me what was left of your corpse. They'd burned and beaten your face until I could hardly recognize you."

Mace gasped, rushed forward, and dropped to her knees at his feet. "Oh my gods. *Garratt*!"

Gar pulled away, moving back as far as the seat would allow. "The Loyalist soldiers were going to take you away to sell you as a sex slave. They shot you when you tried to escape. It *can't* be you."

Mace turned her head, squeezed her eyes shut, and let out a small sob. "I can't believe this."

Faolan cleared his throat and began to back out of the room. "I think I better leave the two of you alone."

Before Gar had a chance to protest, Mace jumped up to pull Faolan back, pushing him down into one of the crew chairs. "Don't you dare move."

"Clearly you two need to talk, pet." Faolan brushed a brown curl from Mace's face. "You don't need me here getting in the way."

"No way, Wolf. I have questions, and I expect answers. Now why the hell didn't you tell me you found my brother? You know I've been looking for him!"

"You said his name was Garratt Simms, not Gar Stitt. How the hell was I supposed to know it was the same man?"

"I changed my name when I thought you were dead. I wanted to forget, start a new life." Gar's stomach churned, and he felt overwhelmed. "I didn't know anyone would be looking for me."

"*I* was looking!"

With his head spinning, Gar chuckled as Mace pouted, her lower lip sticking out as it had when she was ten. He didn't even flinch when she punched him hard on the shoulder.

"Stop it. Ass."

"You haven't changed." He laughed again at the sound of wonder in his own voice. "It's really you. You're alive." He managed to calm himself before the hysteria pulling at his mind gained footing. "How did you escape? Whose body did I see?"

Mace shoved her shoulder into Faolan's body. "Don't know about the body, but our mutual friend here got me out."

Gar turned, his eyes wide. "What?"

Faolan let his gaze travel between the two of them, not stopping even as he reached out to touch each of their cheeks. "How could I not have noticed the similarities before now? You both have the same nose, lips."

He stood quickly, pushing both Gar and Mace away. They waited while Faolan paced, running a hand through his hair to move it from his face. "Kayla and I were on Zeten running a scam on some Loyalist prick. He was bringing in medical supplies cheap, diluting them so he had double the stock to sell before jacking the prices up. We cleaned him out and were fleeing the colony when we found Mace here."

She reached over and squeezed Gar's hand. "I saw the soldiers shoot Dad in the head. When they took me, they told me you were next. I was so scared and angry I fought them. Must have surprised the bastards because the next thing I knew, I broke free and started running."

Gar looked at Faolan, not entirely surprised by the revelation. "You took her with you."

Faolan snorted. "Wasn't about to leave her there. Had we known you were still alive at the time, I would have gone back for you too."

Mace laced her fingers with his. "They told me you were dead, Garratt. It wasn't until a few months later I heard you'd survived. We tried to find you, but it was like you'd fallen off the galactic map."

"I changed my name to hide from the bastards who'd done this. I went to the guild when Jason took over. I wanted to track down the fucker who'd killed you and Dad."

Mace shook her head, brushing a tear from her eye. "All this time lost. How did you—"

"Jason Krieg. He was a Loyalist soldier until he couldn't take it anymore. He was supposed to kill me, but instead smuggled me off the planet."

Faolan frowned. "Shit."

"Yeah. So you can appreciate why I'm a bit confused as to why he wants me dead now. It doesn't make sense."

"It rarely does," Mace whispered.

Gar shook as he sat up straight and pulled his sister into his arms. They clung together, faces buried against each other's necks, tears soaking their clothing. "I missed you." He squeezed her tighter. "I'm so sorry I let you down. You must hate me."

"Don't be an idiot." Mace sat back and grinned. "Why would you possibly think I would hate you? I've spent all this time looking for you. I never stopped."

Gods, he didn't want to do this, not so soon after finding her. "It was my fault."

"What?" Mace dropped her hands to her lap. "How?"

Gar leaned forward, resting his head in his hands. The weight of his guilt from the past decade crashed down on him. "The Loyalist soldiers told me Dad had been wrongly accused. They showed me a document saying he was cleared of Mom's murder and they had the soldier in custody who had done it. I was so excited, I didn't even *think*. I told them where we were hiding Dad. I led them straight home."

The silence in the cabin hurt his ears. It was only slightly more disconcerting than the torrent of images flashing through his memory. The bloody remains of the body had been so disfigured it had been easy to accept it as his sister. Considering the brutal manner in which they'd killed his father, he'd expected no mercy from them at all. As much as he wanted to hide from this, he couldn't. Gar took a breath before looking at his sister.

Mace leaned away, horror and disbelief on her face. "What did you . . .?"

He could feel the renewed tears on his face, but did nothing to wipe away his shame. "I knew better. Dad's life was in danger, and it was my fault they found him."

The sister he never thought he'd see again sat motionless, staring at him. He fought back the impulse to shake a reaction out of her. Instead, he bit down on his bottom lip and waited for her to pass a verdict on his actions.

"I . . . have to go." Mace stood, but he couldn't look at her. "I need time to think. This is all a bit much."

The echo of her retreating footsteps felt like blades tearing his heart apart. He didn't move even once the door closed behind her. The air in the ship was warmer than what he was used to. He really should leave—get back on the *Geilt* and get the hell out of here.

A pair of large hands slid across his shoulders to the back of his neck. "It wasn't your fault."

"Clearly Mace doesn't agree with you."

"She'll be fine if you give her some space. She has you back in her life now, which is something I can confirm she's wanted for a very long time. Come here."

Gar allowed himself to be pulled to his feet. There was no comforting hug this time, only firm hands and gentle guidance. He wanted to protest, but didn't have a clue where they were heading.

"While the family drama has been a nice distraction, we have other matters to attend to."

"Hate to interrupt your schedule, Wolf." Gar finally cleaned his face with the back of his hand, pausing to straighten his tie. He couldn't dwell on what had happened. Either Mace would accept him or he'd go off like he'd originally planned. Either way, he needed Faolan's reassuring presence to help regain his balance. "Think Jason will be able to track us down?"

He followed Faolan into the wide corridor of the ship's main passageway. This ship's appearance was as surprising as its captain and could only be described as homey. Deep reds and blues covered the traditional slate gray in an odd mural pattern.

"Jason will have to pull a tracking miracle out of his ass if he has any hope of finding us. My secure quarters are this way."

A few days ago, Gar going into a notorious pirate's secure quarters would have meant one of them would be a dead man shortly thereafter. Now he found himself looking forward to the promise of solitude.

Funny how difficult prolonged human contact was after being alone for so long.

They stopped and Faolan made introductions to the crew they met on their way. Every time, Gar found himself on the verge of blushing as Faolan's words and the overt flirting directed at him grew. The casual touches increased as well, becoming more possessive if anyone's gaze looked to hold more than a passing interest. Not once in his life had he ever been on the receiving end of this type of attention.

"Here we are." Faolan grinned as they finally reached a large door. A simple palm scan was the only identification needed to trigger access to the room.

Gar shook his head. "Secure quarters, you say."

"Only allows access to certain crew members. That reminds me, if you're staying around, we'll have to make sure we get your prints in the system. Want to make sure you don't get stuck in an inopportune place."

"Like your private quarters?" Gar cocked an eyebrow and smiled.

"I told you they were secure. It prevents people from escaping when I don't want them to." Faolan winked and led the way in.

"You live here?" He tried to take in as many details as possible, nearly overwhelmed by the odd collection of items. Old and new objects from a countless breadth of planets and colonies cluttered the chamber in no obvious semblance of order. Scanners, data chips, and bits of engines were splayed in random piles about the room.

"I sleep here. Occasionally, Mace will come and chat, but mostly this is the lair where the great and mysterious Captain Wolf hides." Faolan snapped his belt off, tossing his sword onto a tabletop covered with datapads. "Speaking of mysterious, let me show you my stone."

"There's a setup if I've ever heard one."

Faolan laughed. "Like I'd ever need a setup to get someone in my bed. They are queuing up for a chance to be with me."

A sickening thought hit Gar, sending a jolt of panic through his body. "You haven't . . . with Mace? Have you?"

Faolan's eyes grew impossibly wide. "With Mace? Gods, she's like a part of my own family. Younger sister I never had. Plus I think she'd cut my balls off if I ever tried anything."

Relief washed through him. "That's good."

"It would have been a bit weird, fucking both brother and sister."

Gar grimaced, not wanting to dwell on the disturbing idea any further. "Stranger things have happened."

Faolan chuckled. "As today has proven. Hang on one minute."

Gar stood in the center of the room—unable to find a clear spot to sit that wasn't the bed—and watched as Faolan pulled a hidden panel from the wall to reveal a safe beneath. Unlike the one on the *Geilt*, this one was comprised of the latest in technology. A quick DNA scan later and the door popped open.

"We raided a known Loyalist cargo transport a month ago. The ship's captain was a bit too willing to part with the things in his hold, which told me there was something more precious hiding on board. I found this in his personal quarters."

Faolan turned around and held up a large emerald stone dangling from the end of a gold chain. It was the most amazing thing Gar had ever laid eyes on. The back of his brain itched, nudging him closer. Stepping forward, he automatically reached for it until Faolan snatched the jewel away, hiding it behind his back.

"It does that to everyone. We've run scan after scan on the bloody thing, but we can't for the life of us figure out how it works." Faolan chuckled as Gar shook his head, clearing the muck away. "It pulls people in, almost compels them to put it on. It's how we discovered the truth about it."

"The mind-reading thing?"

Faolan nodded as he stepped close. "When someone puts the item around their neck, they can read the thoughts of anyone else they focus on. It takes some practice, but Mace and I have both been able to make it work."

Curiosity gnawed at Gar. He wanted to try it out, see exactly how powerful it could be. "Do you think?" He pointed at Faolan's hidden hand. "If you don't mind, that is."

"For you, Stitt?" Faolan stepped up and held the stone between them. "Of course. Let me put it on you."

As Faolan reached behind Gar's neck to fasten the catch, the now-familiar heady musk enveloped Gar. The pang of want unwound once more, tempting him with the promise of closeness and connection. Without thinking, he let his body fall forward until he could rest his forehead on Faolan's shoulder, giving him a better view of his neck. It was only for practicality's sake and had nothing to do with the urge to get closer.

"Have I told you how much I like seeing you like this?" Faolan said softly against his ear.

He shivered. "Like what?"

"Proper, formal, ready to be stripped down and licked from head to toe."

Gar groaned when Faolan stepped out of his grasp.

"Sorry, Stitt, you're going to need to work for the next one."

"Bastard." Gods, it was never enough.

"Already established. Now . . ." Faolan backed up until there was no physical contact between them. "The first time is the hardest. I'll have some random thoughts going on in here, and I want you to try to pick up what I'm saying."

Frowning, Gar reached up and thumbed the stone now resting across his tie. "How do I do that?"

"Concentrate on me. What I'm doing and saying. You'll start to hear a whisper, like someone having a conversation in another room you can barely make out. When the buzzing starts, grab on to it. Those are my thoughts. Okay?"

Gar nodded, not completely convinced, but willing to give it a shot for Faolan. "Go."

Faolan began to chat about his ship, the size of his cargo bay, and the last raid they'd pulled. At first, Gar focused on the words themselves, only to find himself becoming lulled by the sound of the other man's voice.

There!

Something must have shown on his face, because as he looked up, Faolan's smile widened. He continued to speak. Ignoring everything, Gar concentrated on the soft buzzing taking root in the back of his mind. Slowly, it grew, taking shape as a soft murmur, to finally explode into a richer version of Faolan's voice.

I want to strip you naked and suck your cock.

Gar groaned. "Of course it had to be sex with you."

"Is that a no, then?" Faolan laughed and took the opportunity to pull his shirt off. "That was pretty fast for a first try. Better than both of us at least."

"I had a good target." Gar held the stone in the palm of his hand, surprised by the warmth. "Do you have to keep focused on the target?"

Maybe I'll ride you again or let you fuck me in the chair.

"Nope, once you make the connection the stone seems to maintain it. You only need to take the stone off to break it though."

Gar's cock jumped to life at the thoughts now bombarding his brain. "I don't think sex would be a good idea considering you were spacesick just a little over an hour ago."

Not spacesick.

Gar snapped his head up, but Faolan didn't seem to register the thought that had bounced through his mind at hyperspeed pace. The pirate was rummaging through a drawer; he pulled out a black, long-sleeve shirt. Gar knew there was more to things than what Faolan had told him. He relaxed his mind, hoping to pick up another glimpse of what Faolan was hiding.

"I told you it was nothing. Besides, it would be a shame to waste a perfect opportunity like this."

The thought *Want to jerk your cock so I can watch you come* nearly bled over the softer one of *Don't want him to see.* Gar didn't miss it. Faolan didn't realize exactly what was slipping through the cracks and being hauled in by the stone.

"What opportunity is that?" Gar crept closer, making an effort to move slowly while he concentrated on the words. "I've seen your ass, remember?"

"But I haven't shown you all the tricks I can do with that ass. Not to mention the things I can do to yours."

Gods, I want to make him feel so good. I'm hungry.

The utter randomness of the logic jumps were making it difficult for Gar to continue with the conversation. Still, there was something wrong with Faolan, and he wasn't about to let an opportunity to discover what it was slip away. With Faolan now changing his pants, Gar was careful to stay out of his line of sight.

"Well, I don't want to start something, old man, and have you not able to finish. Nothing worse than a lover who runs out of steam halfway through, leaving me to get off on my own."

Won't be there for anyone. Not much longer.

"Shit, Faolan!"

They both froze. Faolan frowned and reached for the stone. Gar moved back, protecting it with his hand. "No."

"What's going on, Gar? Not thinking of running out on me? I'd hate to kill you now."

Better not. Please don't. Mace will hate you.

"I'm not going anywhere until you tell me what's going on." He squeezed the stone until the edges cut into his palm. "What's wrong with you?"

Dying. "There's nothing wrong with me. Now take that bloody thing off."

"What?" The world bottomed out. His knees weakened, and his heart pushed the blood through his body at a maddening pace. "You're . . . what?"

Gar knew the moment Faolan realized he'd screwed up. Faolan closed his eyes, smiling softly. "Gar, don't do this."

"No! After everything that's passed between us, everything that's happened today with Mace, I think I've earned the right to know. Now tell me."

Faolan sighed. *I'm dying.* "Sorry. I'm so sorry."

TWELVE

"**P**lease, Gar, take the stone off and we'll talk."

Faolan wasn't exactly sure what he'd let slip through to get them to this point, but he didn't want to have this conversation and be at an unfair disadvantage. Really, he was surprised this hadn't happened sooner in his earlier tests with Mace. He'd been too busy flirting, too cocky in his ability to control his thoughts and feelings, and had forgotten that Gar brought out another side of him. Things were still new, untested, and now the fragile relationship they'd somehow built was in danger of shattering.

Without further prompting, Gar reached behind his neck and undid the chain's clasp. He held out the stone, his hand trembling slightly as he waited for Faolan to reclaim his prize.

"Thanks." Faolan was careful to only touch the chain. "I'll just put this away and then we can discuss things."

It only bought him a little bit of time, but he planned on using every second he could to collect his thoughts. This really shouldn't be a difficult task. Gar wasn't as close to him as Mace or the rest of the crew were. Their few days together, although giving Faolan some of the best sex he'd had in years, shouldn't mean anything more to him than a casual encounter he could easily walk away from.

He couldn't.

"Mind if I sit?" He sauntered over to his chair, pushed the pile of clothing on top of it to the floor, and sank down into it. "I need to know exactly what you heard."

Gar continued to stand in the middle of the room. He wasn't looking at any one particular thing, but Faolan was sad to note Gar's gaze didn't come his way either.

"You said you were dying."

Idiot. "We're all dying in one way or another. You know that."

"Faolan, don't." Gar's voice lacked all of his normal self-confidence, and his blue eyes had grown impossibly wide. "Just tell me what is going on."

He didn't want to say the words, knowing the moment he did, it would make them true. He'd been fighting it for so long, the illusion of health giving him strength to continue.

"Last year I pulled a scam on one of the Loyalist colonial administrators. It was simple. Go in posing as an outlander colonist security detail, make some offers of providing information, and snatch a cache of ID datapads on the way out the door. What I hadn't realized was the bastard recognized me from one of the security bulletins a few months earlier."

Gar's eyes closed. "Shit."

"To put it mildly. He poisoned my food. Small dose, just enough to put me out of commission long enough so he could collect the bounty on my head—and more than enough to leave my immune system in shreds." Faolan finally looked away from the pained expression on Gar's face to study his lifeline. "I've been taking what meds I can find here and there to prolong things, but I'm fighting a losing battle."

"Is there a cure?"

He ignored the heavy emotion in Gar's voice. "Probably, but I'll be damned if I can find one. It's not like I have access to the best doctors the Loyalist colonies have to offer."

"And the man?"

"Dead. Was killed when Ricco came in and saved me."

"Good."

A rustle of clothing, and before he realized, Gar was by his side, running a hand through his hair. The strong fingers felt good on his scalp, so he selfishly leaned in.

"How long do you have?"

"That's what I like about you, Stitt. You cut to the chase and ask what's on your mind."

Fingers tightened in his hair, tugging his head back until he had no choice but to look into Gar's light-blue eyes.

"How long?"

"If I can find more meds, maybe a year. Less if I can't. I was going to use the money from the stone to buy up what I could and give the remainder to the crew."

"Do they know?" Gar moved his hand down to rest it on the back of Faolan's neck. The possessiveness of his touch made Faolan shiver. "Is this why you were so tired on my ship?"

"No and yes. I usually have a good period after I've taken the serum, but it's been getting shorter and shorter."

The gentle rubbing of Gar's thumb on his skin eased the tension of his muscles. The weight of his secret, while not completely gone, lifted enough that he was able to breathe. Gar knew, and he hadn't freaked out or run away. It had to count for something.

"Is there anything I can do to help?" Gar bent over and pressed a kiss to his temple. "I can take the *Geilt* out and see if I can find more of the drugs you need. Or track down a buyer for the stone, if that would help."

Lifting his head, Faolan enjoyed the brush of skin on skin as he rubbed his nose against Gar's stubbled cheek. It figured his life was at an end just as he found someone he could live for. "I'm fine."

"Stubborn ass, you're not. A slow death by poisoning is not *fine*. You need help. Let me be the one. I don't know how yet, but I'll find a way to make this right. But you're going to have to trust me."

Gar dropped to his knees and wrapped him in a hug. He fought the embrace for a moment until he realized Gar wasn't about to let go. It was okay to give in to the comfort being offered. He could take refuge with a man who barely knew him, and it would be okay. He didn't have to be strong all the time. For some strange reason, the universe crossed their paths when he needed it the most—giving him something to hold on to as the darkness encroached.

Turning his face into Gar's neck, he let out a soft sigh. "Thank you."

"I know neither one of us do whatever the hell *this* is, but I've never been one to walk away from a friend."

Faolan chuckled, squeezing Gar tighter. "I'm a friend, am I? We've known each other three days."

"You're forgetting something." Gar pulled back but didn't release him. "I'm trained to size a person up in a matter of minutes. I can tell if someone is lying or is the genuine deal. I've spent more time with you in the last few days than I have with anyone outside of my family."

"That's not saying much for your life, Stitt."

Gar smiled, sitting back on his feet. "No, it's not."

Faolan studied his new lover and tried to imagine the life Gar had been forced to lead since the death of his father. Believing his sister was dead, knowing his innocent actions resulted in such heartache. Faolan was surprised the man wasn't more damaged than he was.

Still, here sat a man who, despite the shit storm of his life, wasn't afraid to take a chance on him. Gar was willing to risk everything in a futile attempt to find a cure that in all likelihood didn't exist. Faolan knew he didn't deserve a man like that in his life, but he was selfish enough not to turn him away.

"You're something else, Gar." Faolan watched as a shudder passed through Gar. "What?"

"I don't know why you . . . I've never felt like this about anyone. I can't believe I've only known you for such a short time." Frowning, Gar pulled away before smoothing down his tie. "Do you believe in an instant connection between people?"

"Yes." He didn't need further explanation to know what Gar was trying to ask. "Yes, I do."

"How can you be sure it's real? How do you know you're not imagining something that isn't there just to ease . . . just so you're not so . . ."

"Alone?"

Gar nodded.

"I mentioned my late wife, yes?"

Gar nodded again. "How long has she been gone?"

"Ten years." The pain may have been over a decade old, but Faolan knew the ache in his heart would never completely go away. "It was a few months after we pulled Mace off Zeten."

Gar's lips twitched. Faolan wasn't sure if he was fighting a smile or a grimace.

"I never did have a chance to thank you for saving my sister."

Faolan waved the praise aside. "Anyone would have done the same thing given the situation. It's not like your home rock is the nicest place in the universe to live."

"Still, thanks." Gar rose to his feet and made his way over to the bed. "Your wife?"

Faolan leaned back in his seat and let Kayla's memory wash over him. "When I first laid eyes on her, I knew she was meant to be with me. All she did was walk into the room and I knew I'd never love another woman. We weren't apart until the day she died. She was amazing. Kayla could strip any security system on a ship or base before the owner even knew she was there. Gods, she was beautiful, but had a mean streak in her when she thought someone was being an ass. It was what got her killed in the end."

Gar didn't say anything, only sat there with his hands folded in his lap and waited. It had been such a long time since anyone was there for him, Faolan had forgotten what it felt like, the rush of emotions as they poured from the secret place he kept buried. It burned and liberated all at once.

"We heard about a man on one of the new outland colonies who was stealing organs from the unfortunate and selling them to the highest bidder back in the Loyalist colonies. I didn't want to touch it, but Kayla was on fire, wanted to make the bastard pay. The Loyalists blew up her ship before they got close to the planet. Killed Kayla and her crew."

"I'm sorry."

The old guilt reared up and bit at his conscience. "I should have gone with her. Maybe I would have noticed they'd been picked up by sensors and been able to save them all."

"Or maybe you would have died with her. You can't second-guess your actions, Faolan."

"Like you are?"

He knew he'd made a direct hit when Gar flinched.

"That's different."

"How old were you again?"

"That's not the—"

"How old?"

"Fourteen."

"So you're saying I'm not responsible for my actions as a twenty-two-year-old man, but you are when you were nothing more than a child?"

"It's not the same."

"Of course it's the same. We're too much alike, Stitt."

He saw the flash of realization wash over Gar. The turmoil of emotions swirled in the bounty hunter's too bright gaze as old emotions surfaced and were dealt with.

"You said the good periods are getting shorter for you." Gar rubbed the back of his neck. "Do you have any more of the meds to take?"

"I have a few doses left. They're pretty weak though, old stock. Potency isn't what it should be." He winked at Gar and threw him his best leer. "Don't worry, I'll still be good to you for a month or so yet."

"You are unbelievable." Gar fell back on the bed and pressed the heels of his hands to his eyes. "You've just told me you're dying, and you honestly think I care about whether or not I can still have sex with you?"

Faolan stood and walked over to the small washing room off the sleeping quarters. Only a fraction of the size of the one on the *Geilt*, it still had room for everything Faolan needed. He knew Gar was watching him, but did nothing to conceal his actions. He grabbed the med spray from where it sat on the shelf.

"When I bought these meds a few months back, the medic told me they weren't the right ones. It would help with the symptoms only, push off the worst, temporarily repair some of what the poison had damaged." He pressed the needle to his neck and waited for the rush as the meds hit his bloodstream. "Apparently there are better options, but as I said, nothing a pirate like me would have access to. Loyalist poison, Loyalist cure."

"What do you plan to do?"

There were so many answers Faolan could give him. Distractions and pretty evasions were easy enough for a mind like his to manufacture. The truth was a much different matter. With Gar, he found himself needing to open up. As much as he wanted to break through Gar's protective shell, the desire to show him how alike they really were was greater.

"I'm going to enjoy what time I have left and find happiness where I can."

Gar stood, hesitated for a moment, and approached Faolan. He didn't move, waiting to see what Gar would do. Their eyes met in the mirror, neither looking away. It was amazing how Faolan's opinion of Gar had changed. Faolan knew he wasn't the cold tight-ass apparent on first impression. Gar's passions ran deep, held in check by his need to protect what remained of his heart. Faolan understood that need—he'd sunk so low after Kayla, he'd never imagined he could love anyone else again.

Not until now.

"We're on your ship, Wolf. Do the others need you?"

Gar didn't wait for an answer, but undid the buttons of his jacket and vest, slipped them off, and hung them from the clothing hook.

"I think I can claim captain's prerogative and hide out for an hour or so."

Gar cocked his head and smiled. "If you need to give them directives, I suggest you do it now."

"Oh?"

"You're about to become indisposed for the next little while, Wolf."

"Bossy." Faolan grinned. "I like that."

"You'll like it even more once you know what I have planned."

Faolan's grin widened. "Sounds good." As he reached for the com control, a loud alarm filled the room. "Shit. That's the defense perimeter alarm. We're under attack."

He didn't wait to see if Gar followed, but pushed past him, running for the door. The crew were rushing to their stations, shoving past anyone who slowed them down. For the first time in days, Faolan felt his head even and clear as he jogged to the bridge. The meds might not be completely potent, but they did the trick.

"Status report," he barked at Mace, who sat in his chair.

"What's he doing here?" She pointed at Gar who strode in a half second behind him, clothing as proper as it had been before he'd entered Faolan's quarters.

"I'm here to help, Macie." Gar spoke softly, but his voice carried clearly over the noise.

"I trust him as much as I do any of you." Faolan pointedly looked around the room, finally letting his gaze land on Mace. "He deserves the same chance I give everyone who joins my crew. Considering your varied backgrounds, I'd think everyone here would agree."

No one said anything. Even Mace looked suitably chastised, which in itself was a small miracle. Striding across the room, he waited for Mace to move before falling into his chair.

"Now last time I checked, I was still the captain of this bucket. Someone give me a status!"

"Captain," Mace said, her eyes locked on Gar. "Three Loyalist raiders just jumped through the gate and are on an intercept course for us. I've set our trajectory for the gas giant."

"Good thinking, Mace." Faolan checked the readings being fed to his console. "We identify these boys yet?"

Dragan spoke up from weapons control. "Transponders are the same as the convoy we hit six months ago. We stripped them of the *euridian* ore."

"Time to intercept?" With their recent use of the dimension jump drive, they had lost that quick escape option; the device took a full standard day to recharge.

"Not long." Mace shifted and took her seat at navigation. "Ten minutes max."

"Time to the gas giant?"

Mace grimaced. "At least fifteen."

Damn it. "Okay, people, let's be sharp. Weapons on full, shields up. They are going to hit us hard."

"What can I do?"

Faolan looked at Gar, suddenly at a loss for how he could help. "We don't have an open station. Just hold on and let me know if you see anything odd."

Gar shook his head. "Let me take the *Geilt* out. Two targets are harder than one. I can draw their fire and slow them down."

Ricco spun in his seat. "Bad idea. For all we know, he's working with them."

Before Faolan could respond, Mace threw a datapad at Ricco. "Shut it, Terrin. My brother's no Loyalist."

Every head in the room snapped around to stare. Mouth gaping, Ricco tried to stutter out an answer.

"Enough!" Faolan sat straight in his chair. "We don't have time for the family dramatics with three Loyalist cruisers breathing down our necks." Taking a deep breath, he faced Gar. "You sure the *Geilt* can handle ships that large?"

Gar snorted. "Please. They'd have to catch me first."

Somewhere deep in his gut, Faolan didn't want to let him go. Here on the *Belle Kurve*, Gar was as safe as Faolan could make him. Faolan could control the situation and offer more protection than the personal cruiser ever could. Still, two targets would buy them the time they needed to take out the superior foe. It was the right call, but it didn't mean he had to like it.

"Go." His stomach rolled. "And be careful."

"You too." Gar's lips twitched into a lopsided smile before he turned and ran.

"Okay, Mace, we're going to have to slow down enough to let the *Geilt* get free of our clamps. But I don't want it to let us get within weapons range any faster than we need to."

Mace tapped her fingers along the edge of the computer controls. "We can slingshot him around, throw him clear and confuse the hell out of them. It will only force us to reduce speed by three *keagans* and will give Gar one hell of a rush."

"Think you can handle that?"

Mace rolled her eyes, and Faolan had to smile at the family trait. "Please, I could do it in my sleep."

He counted to thirty in his head before signaling the *Geilt*. "Stitt, you in place?"

"Hatch secured and I'm ready to go."

Mace cracked her knuckles as she got into position. "Okay, big brother, I hope you're as good as your reputation says you are."

It might not have been obvious to others, but Faolan picked up on the change in Mace's tone. The undertones of forgiveness. *Thank the gods.*

"I'm better. What do you have in mind?"

The plan was hashed out between the two siblings with little input from others. Faolan had to admire the sharp minds they both possessed, their natural affinity for tactics, and their shrewd battle senses. This was going to be fun.

The ship's proximity alarms sounded, telling them the cruisers were in missile range. "Here we go, people. Stay sharp!"

Far faster than he'd anticipated, the ships closed on the *Belle Kurve*, breaking formation to reform in a triangular attack strike. Mace pushed the ship's engines to maximum, racing them directly toward the gas giant.

"Ready, Garratt?" Mace's hand hovered above the release button.

"Let me go, Macie."

There was a ship-wide shudder as the *Geilt* broke free and the *Belle Kurve* veered off in the opposite direction. One target became two, forcing the Loyalist ships to slow their pursuit.

"Dragan, hit the ship closest with missiles and the next one with lasers. Stitt?"

Gar's voice crackled through the com as the *Geilt*'s shield absorbed a laser blast. "I've got the third one. Will have his shields down momentarily."

Another powerful shudder rattled the hull, sending Faolan bouncing in his seat. "Open up on them. Everything we have!"

The battle quickly became a blur of lasers, voices, and missile barrages. Faolan's voice grew raw from the litany of commands he barked at his crew, the muscles of his neck and back screaming from discomfort and tension. It took far longer than he would have liked to finally disable one of the Loyalist ships.

"Yes!" Dragan jumped to his feet, punching the air.

"Sit your ass down, rookie," Mace yelled at him. "We're not out of this yet."

"Yes, ma'am."

"Smart boy." Faolan winked at his second-in-command. "He knows not to piss the lady off."

The *Belle Kurve* rattled again. Faolan looked up in time to see the smallest of the Loyalist cruisers explode.

Gar's even voice broke through the communication system. "Target dealt with."

"Last one is ours, Stitt." Faolan leaned forward, resting his elbows on his knees. "Unless you want a piece?"

"I normally keep my toys to myself. In this case, more than happy to share."

Mace chuckled as she brought the ship around. "Sarcastic bastard."

"Hey, he's your family." Faolan grinned. "Let's clean up this mess and bring him back in."

As Mace finished the loop, now head-on with the Loyalist, Gar shifted the *Geilt* so he approached the enemy on a perpendicular vector. Lasers blazing, they unloaded everything they had on the target. Sensors beeped a warning.

"Mace, pull us out of here. She's going to blow." Faolan signaled Gar. "Stitt, fall back. You're going to get caught in the blast radius." Static answered him. "Stitt?"

The Loyalist cruiser exploded, sending metal racing toward the *Geilt*, which was still far too close for safety. Faolan was on his feet and by Mace's seat without thinking.

"Readings?" His voice was ragged even to his own ears.

"Oh gods. No. Direct hit to his hull. Shields are down."

"Get us over there."

"I'm trying," she spat back. "There's too much debris to move in safely."

The com crackled, then the frequency resolved and Gar's voice came through again. "*Belle Kurve*, hold your position."

Faolan laughed, ignoring the sudden rush of tears to his eyes. "Stitt, you better not blame me for damaging your ship."

"Not safe yet. Hold your position and get ready to scoop me up if necessary."

Faolan watched, helpless, as Gar maneuvered the *Geilt* away from the splintering Loyalist hulk and back to safety. He didn't realize how tensely he'd been holding his body until he felt Mace reach up and cover his hand with hers.

"He'll be okay," she said softly.

Unwilling to let even Mace see the depth of his feelings, he scoffed, squeezing her hand back. "Of course he will be. Your brother is a stubborn ass."

"Like a certain captain I know."

"Don't tell Gar. He may not want to come back on board."

Mace stared up at him. "You really like him, don't you?"

He kept looking at the *Geilt*. "You know, Mace, I think maybe I might—"

The words died in Faolan's mouth as a secondary explosion split a chunk of drifting hull into small fragments. They were too close to the *Geilt*, making it nearly impossible for Gar to steer free.

"Gar, look out!" he shouted, knowing it was pointless.

He stood there and watched as the debris collided with the side of the *Geilt*'s hull.

CHAPTER
THIRTEEN

"**G**ar, look out!"

Well, what the bloody hell else am I going to do? With no time to respond, Gar threw as much power as he could afford into what remained of his shields, squeezed his eyes shut, and braced for impact.

The barrage of metal from the Loyalist cruiser beat through the meager remains of the *Geilt*'s shields to slam into the hull. The vibrations shook the ship so hard Gar fell to the floor, slamming his head on the edge of the chair.

Blackness quickly followed him as the chaos was silenced.

Gar wasn't sure what happened next, and could only hear snatches of noises as he fought through the mental fog.

"Fire here!"

He tried to move, but a weight pressed on his chest. His eyes refused to cooperate, so he gave up trying to open them.

"Find . . . near . . . cockpit."

Who was that? The voice sounded strikingly familiar, but an image of the owner escaped his wounded mind.

"Turn that noise off!"

The voice was close, almost on top of him. He couldn't sit up. Struggling, he managed to move his hand free from beneath the weight on top of him.

"Help." He couldn't be sure if he'd actually spoken, so Gar swallowed and tried again. "Help." Louder, clearer, and this time garnering a reaction.

"Shut up, everyone, and let me listen." Faolan's voice. He'd come for him.

"Help."

"Oh my gods, Garratt. Here! He's over here, Faolan."

He felt hands on his body as voices rang around him. One in particular soothed him, so he reached out for it.

"Hey, hey, don't do that." Warm lips kissed his forehead. "Lie still while we dig you out."

"Faolan?"

"See, Mace. Even with a blow to the head I'm completely unforgettable."

Gar wanted to laugh at the teasing arrogance, but the pain in his chest prevented it. "Ass," he whispered.

"I'm the ass? I thought I told you to watch out?"

"Tried."

"Well, next time try harder. Took us over an hour to get to you. I wasn't sure if this ship of yours would hold together that long."

"Okay."

Another kiss, this time to his lips. "What have I told you about these single-word sentences? We still need to work on that."

"Don't . . . want . . ."

"Will you stop goading him?" Mace's voice. "Just ignore him, Garratt."

"Gar," he croaked.

"What?"

"Gar . . . now."

"I'll call you whatever the hell you want as long as you shut up and let us dig you out. Keep him still, Faolan. Doc says to try to keep him awake too. He probably has a concussion."

"That means I get to talk to you." Faolan shifted so his lips now hovered beside Gar's ear. "I can tell you all the dirty little things I plan to do to you when you're safe and sound."

Faolan's rich voice lulled the panic threatening to rise in Gar. While the litany of sexual positions would normally arouse him beyond reason, at the moment it served to keep him in the present. After a few minutes, Faolan's list changed focus. The vulgar language melted into promises of properly cooked meals and rest on a comfortable bed if Gar would simply hold on and get better. His brain clung to the fact Faolan wanted him. Really, honestly wanted *him* to be around.

Gods, he wished his eyes would cooperate and let him see Faolan. Just one more time . . .

There was a pause in the shuffle around him, a soft mutter of whispers too gentle for his abused ears. Faolan shifted, knees cradling Gar's head, and looped both his hands under Gar's shoulders.

"Okay, Gar. We're going to get this sheeting off you now. The boys are going to lift it up, and I'm going to pull you out. Just hold on and this will be all over soon."

"Hurts." His tongue was heavy and too thick in his mouth, making speech difficult.

"It will be all over very soon." Another kiss against his forehead. "Okay everyone, let's do this on three."

He counted along with Faolan silently in his head, bracing himself for the inevitable pain he'd feel. It was worse than he could have imagined. A scream ripped from him as Faolan jerked him free. The majority of the pain emanated from his right leg and sent him scrambling to try to cover the wound with his hand. Too much, it was all too much.

"Gods, lie still, Stitt." Faolan tightened his grip on his shoulders. "Mace, sedate him before he damages something Doc can't fix."

Gar thrashed, trying to bat them away. "No, no, no, no." The needle sank into his arm and blackness overtook his will to stay conscious.

Gar's hearing returned before anything else. It was surreal to figure out his surroundings when all he had to rely on was the steady beep of a computer and an annoying ringing he couldn't be sure was real or inside his head.

Slowly, his brain acknowledged the warmth of a blanket covering his body, a pillow that had grown lopsided from the weight of his head, and a large, warm hand holding his.

"Ouch," he whispered.

"Let that be a lesson to you." There was no mistaking the relief in Faolan's voice.

"What's that?"

"When you try to be the hero, bad things happen."

"I'll . . . keep that in mind."

Without opening his eyes, Gar tried to adjust his body so he was elevated more, only to be stopped by Faolan. "Don't think so, Stitt. Doc said if you moved too soon, the tissue regeneration for your leg won't heal properly."

Cracking an eye open, Gar grimaced at the strength of the lights. Faolan reached over and dimmed them, allowing Gar to see for the first time in what felt like an eternity.

He looked at Faolan, not down at his own battered body. "How bad?"

"Do you want some water? Hungry? I can get Mace to bring something for you if you want."

"Faolan." It never boded well when distraction was the first tactic used. "How bad?"

Faolan stared at him hard, the muscles in his jaw and neck working overtime. Finally, he reached out and cupped Gar's cheek with his hand. "Came close to losing you. Somehow Doc pulled out a miracle and patched you up. Claimed you're only alive because you're one stubborn bastard."

Fear hit Gar like a punch to the gut. He'd been given a tremendous opportunity over the past day, and he'd almost died before he'd had a chance to reacquaint himself with his sister. Then there was Faolan.

"You know me," Gar smiled, "I'm not about to let anyone dictate what I should do. Even die."

"Good man." Faolan rubbed his thumb over Gar's cheek in a steady rhythm. "I was just getting used to having you around."

"Can I . . .?" Gar nodded at the glass of water sitting beside Faolan. "Guess I was thirsty after all."

"You'll learn to listen to me." Faolan held the straw up to Gar's lips, not letting him take too much. "Everyone does in the end."

Gar waited for Faolan to put the glass down before reaching out to take his hand. "There are benefits to it, I'm thinking. You gave me quite the list to ponder back on the *Geilt*."

For the first time since Gar had met him, Faolan blushed. "Ah, that. Well, I was just saying whatever came to mind. Figured you're a guy, sex was the easiest thing to focus on. It's not like I was about to run over a list of damages with you."

He didn't want to push things and bring up the *other* items Faolan had mentioned. Best for them both to keep the conversation on safe topics until they had time to work through exactly what it was between them.

"Speaking of the *Geilt*: how bad is my ship?"

Faolan winced. "Better than you, but still pretty beat up. It took us a bit, but we managed to get her tethered to the *Belle Kurve* and are en route to a safe port. We'll be able to get to work on her soon enough."

The thought of his ship damaged hurt more than his leg. He'd invested so much of his life in it, the *Geilt* had become more than simple transport. It was his home.

"I did get this out for you." Faolan winked and dug in his pocket for a moment before pulling out an object.

"Dad's stopwatch." Gar took it, hands shaking.

"The safe busted open. I knew it was important, so . . ." Faolan shrugged.

"Thanks." Gar swallowed, doing his best to ignore the lump forming in his throat. "Mace will probably want to see it."

"Now you can show her yourself. It's almost time for her to come down and take over Gar duty. I should let Doc know you're awake too. She'll want to examine you, make sure that thick skull of yours is in good shape."

Faolan stood, but Gar caught his hand, stopping him from leaving. "You'll be back later?"

He knew he shouldn't sound so pathetic and needy, his desires barely concealed. He was tired of doing what others wanted or what he thought was right. For once in his life he was going to reach out and take something for purely selfish reasons.

Right now, he wanted Faolan for as long as he could have him.

"Once I know you're okay and your sister has had a chance to reassure herself you're alive, I'll be back."

Faolan bent down and kissed his cheek.

Fuck that. Snaking his hand around the back of Faolan's neck, Gar directed him to his lips. The kiss was gentle, full of purpose and passion. The pain from his leg prevented his cock from responding, but Gar knew he'd have a raging hard-on when he thought back on this moment.

"I'm going to hold you to every item on that list," he whispered against Faolan's lips.

"Good." Faolan threaded his fingers through Gar's hair. "Good."

A yawn slipped through Gar's defenses. "I'm just going to close my eyes for a bit."

"Get some sleep and don't let Mace wear you out when she stops by."

"Come back when you can, Captain."

Faolan winked before striding out the door. Gar watched as he went, drawn to the way Faolan moved, the confident stride and very firm ass. He liked that ass a bit more than he should.

The stopwatch in his hand grew warm as he clutched it tightly to his chest. Of all the things Faolan could have taken from his ship, the items easily slipped away to be sold or used at a later time, he brought the one thing he knew was special to Gar. Kept it safe until Gar could reclaim it. Rolling over, Gar smiled. Sleep took him then, as dreams of strong hands and laughter filled his mind.

"I don't care what you say, Doc. It's not normal for a man his age to be sleeping this much."

Gar cracked a single eye open to see Mace standing there, hands on hips, glaring at an older woman he assumed was Doc.

"It is perfectly normal when the man in question had a giant piece of metal sheeting fall on his body and tear his leg up." Doc snapped Mace on the end of her nose. "And don't think just because the captain promoted you to second-in-command you can come in here and tell me how to do my job."

"He's my brother."

"He's my patient."

"Gods save me from the pair of you."

"Gar!" Mace grinned, pulling him up into a crushing hug. "I didn't know you were awake."

"How could I sleep with you bitching and complaining?"

She smacked him hard in the shoulder. "Bastard."

"Please no hitting my patient, Ms. Simms. Not until I've had a chance to look him over. How are you feeling, Mr. Stitt?"

"Leg hurts. Back hurts. Chest throbs."

Doc tapped her finger on the computer monitor. "Good. All as it should be."

Mace snorted. "Pain is as it should be?"

"Your brother had half a ship fall on him. He's very fortunate he can feel anything at all and isn't lying there paralyzed." She typed in a few more commands, and Gar was overtaken by a rush of euphoric numbness. "There we go."

"Wow." He examined the tips of his fingers, fascinated by the sudden tingle. "What was that?"

"Painkiller. Some nice drugs the captain drummed up from a Loyalist colony a few months back. Good to know they work as intended."

"Am I going to be able to talk to him?" Mace took the chair beside his bed. Gar picked up her hand and started poking the tips of her fingers. "Or is he a drugged-out mess now?"

"Talk, but he'll sleep again soon."

Gar only noticed Doc had left when the *whoosh* of the door closing caught his attention. "She's nice."

Mace chuckled. "You're only saying that because she gave you the good drugs."

"She likes me." He grinned.

"No, she likes Faolan and Faolan likes you."

"I like Faolan." Somewhere in the back of his mind, Gar registered what he'd said. Normally, he'd die before confessing anything remotely close to his true feelings. It didn't matter Mace was the only family he had—Gar's feelings were his alone. The drugs must have been stronger than he realized.

"You do?" Mace brushed the hair from his forehead, making him feel cooler. "You just met him though."

"I'm lonely. Faolan makes me smile."

Mace opened her mouth to say something, then snapped it shut before frowning and trying again. "So you've been on your own since leaving Zeten?"

He nodded, liking the dizzy rush the motion caused. "I'm not good for anyone. Hurt you and Dad. Jason didn't want me around. Scared I'd hurt him too."

"You're not scared you're going to hurt Faolan?"

When he shook his head, Gar did it a bit too fast, causing his stomach to flip in a nauseous spin. "He's . . . No, won't hurt him."

"Okay, settle down." Mace cooed at him, rubbing the back of his hand and forearm until his panic began to subside. "Sorry, big brother. I guess those drugs are stronger than the Doc gave them credit for."

Sighing, Gar turned until he could hug Mace's arm. "Missed you, Macie."

"I missed you too, Gar. Get some rest."

"Don't be mad at me."

He drifted off to sleep without hearing her response.

Gar woke up alone. With his mind clear of drugs, the ache from his body was strong but manageable. Surprised he'd been left on his own, he pushed himself to a sitting position high enough not to choke on the water he greedily gulped. His memories of the past little while were fuzzy. Vague recollections of Faolan and Mace bled together until he wasn't sure if they were all true or manufactured fantasies.

Gods, he wasn't even sure of the date.

Reaching over, he tried to press the computer display, but only managed to knock over his water glass. "Shit."

It was at that moment Faolan chose to walk into the room. "What the hell are you doing?"

"Wanted to see what the star date is. Guess I'm still not coordinated."

"Well, you're certainly more coherent than the last time I saw you. Turns out there was a bit of a truth serum mixed in with the pain meds. Fun people, those Loyalists."

Foggy recollection of a conversation with Mace crept up to the forefront of his mind. "I hope you didn't take advantage, Wolf."

Faolan grinned. "I would never dream of it. Though I have to admit you were quite the conversationalist. My cock was stiff and sore from listening to that accent of yours."

Gar groaned and buried his face in his hands. "I hate you."

"If by 'hate' you mean you can't get enough of my big hands and tight ass, then I hate you too."

Gar began to chuckle, only to have it turn into a full-out laugh that was quickly joined by Faolan's. "And to answer your earlier question, you've been in my med bay for just over a week."

All amusement fell away from Gar. "Gods."

Faolan's gaze roamed over Gar's body; the white medical gown did very little to conceal his chest. "I was scared you weren't going to get out of bed again. Doc checked your latest scans, and she thinks you'll be able to move to private quarters later today if you're up for it."

Something in the way Faolan spoke grabbed Gar's attention. "Do you have spare quarters?"

"We do, but they're not very big." Faolan sat on the edge of the bed and smoothed down the blanket bunched around Gar's waist. "Of course, my quarters would be ideal for you until the *Geilt* is livable again."

Stunned didn't do Gar's feelings justice. "You want me to live in your quarters?"

"Just until you're back on your feet. Don't get any ideas about this being a permanent arrangement, hunter."

"Wouldn't dream of it." He wasn't about to tell Faolan how relieved he was simply to stay on the *Belle Kurve*. The idea of going back to a solitary existence terrified him. Staying in the captain's quarters—more time getting to know Faolan—was a bonus.

"Good." Faolan shifted his hand so it rested on Gar's thigh just below his wound.

Gar's skin itched where the graft was healing under the layers of bandages. He scratched at it through the coverings, wishing he was completely recovered. His fingers brushed Faolan's, pulling a gasp from both of them. The look in Faolan's eyes sent a shiver through Gar's body, straight to his cock.

"Today?" He entwined his fingers with Faolan's.

"Right now if you want. I can pull some strings. I know the captain."

"I hear he's a bastard."

"Only to people who've pissed him off."

Gar bit his lower lip. "Are you sure you want to do this? Have me around all the time?"

"It's just until you're back on your feet." Faolan squeezed his thigh gently. "I mean, I know you'd do the same for me."

"Yeah, of course. It really shouldn't be very long at all."

"Nope, you'll be walking around being a pain in the ass in no time."

"And it will be a good chance for us to work out a plan for you to sell the stone."

Faolan stood, grinning. "See, I knew this was a great idea. I'll let Doc know."

"Fantastic." Gar's cheeks ached from the strain of his smile.

He wanted nothing more than to be closer to Faolan, to have the opportunity to learn everything there was to know about the pirate. His blood hummed as it raced through his body, the promise of happiness within his reach. All he had to do was not screw it up.

He could do that. He hoped.

CHAPTER
FOURTEEN

"This was a mistake."

Gar swung his legs over the side of the bed and tried to escape Faolan's grasp before he was mothered to death. If the week in the med bay had been a haze of want and half memories, the following week in Faolan's quarters was the crystal-clear realization of how different they really were.

He'd tried to relax and let Faolan look after him, but he wasn't used to having every detail of his life managed. Gods, he wasn't a child in need of care. He'd survived the worst situation imaginable and come out the other side stronger for the experience. Maybe Faolan's care and constant touches were a byproduct of the pirate's own loneliness, something he tried his hardest to hide from others.

It was more than apparent to Gar.

"I told you not to push yourself as hard as you were." Faolan sighed on his way to snatch a glass of Terrin brandy. Hating himself a little, Gar couldn't help staring at the roll of muscles as Faolan swallowed the drink down. "Doc only gave you the all clear a few days ago. You can't expect us to find you something to do on the ship right away. Plus, you're getting stronger every day. Why not sit back and rest up?"

He'd honestly tried to make it work between them . . . whatever the hell it was. Lust for sure, but Gar knew something else was trying to build. He wasn't about to put a label on it, as nothing good would come of that. Separation would give him the perspective necessary to figure out his feelings and exactly what he wanted to do about them.

"I'm not talking about working on your ship." He didn't want to have this conversation. Not after everything Faolan had done to help him. Squeezing his knees as hard as his injury would allow, he fought to keep his voice even. "I'm talking about me staying here with you."

The hollow echo of the glass being set down heavily on the table filled the room. "What?"

Smooth, Gar. "It's been a long time since I've been with anyone for an extended period of time. Hell, you've been around me consecutively longer in three weeks than Jason had for the past three years."

"And that's a bad thing?"

He knew Faolan didn't understand his desire for solitude. If Gar had learned nothing else about the man over the past few weeks, it was his need for constant companionship. Not that Faolan was any more forthcoming with the personal information than Gar, but he seemed to thrive having people cling to his side.

It drove Gar insane. "I think I'll move back to the *Geilt.*"

"It's in no condition for you to be living there. *You're* in no condition to be living there. What if there's a problem and you need Doc?"

"The *Geilt* is tethered to your ship. Not exactly a long distance or far-flung galaxy. If I need Doc she can get to me fast enough."

Faolan crossed his arms and widened his stance. Gar now knew this was his typical *I'm the captain and you damn well better listen to me* pose. "I'm not going to risk the well-being of my crew to accommodate an asinine request."

Gar cocked an eyebrow. "Excuse me? Not a member of your crew, Wolf."

Faolan waved the protest away. "Of course you are. Jason betrayed you, where else will you go? You'll stay with us."

Of all the conceited, arrogant presumptions. "I prefer to be on my own."

Faolan opened his mouth to respond, paused, and snapped it shut. He poured another two fingers of the brandy, downing it in one gulp. "No one should be alone, Gar. Not even you. *Especially* not you."

Dropping his chin to his chest, Gar sighed. "You presume to know me very well."

"Better than you think."

"I'm not like you, Wolf." Two different men from two very different backgrounds. He wasn't sure if he could take the step forward necessary to bridge the gap, to take them to a place beyond friendship. "I'm too used to being on my own."

Faolan tapped the tabletop with his finger before pulling his shirt off and padding barefoot over to the bed. He didn't reach for Gar or make any move to sit beside him—he stood and waited, hands on hips.

"What?" Gar asked when he couldn't take the unusual silence any longer.

"How are we different?"

What the hell? "Do you want a detailed description or will a short list be sufficient?"

Faolan frowned. "Shut up and listen for once. I asked you a simple question. Answer it."

"I don't understand." They didn't have even a passing resemblance.

"Look at me." Faolan held his arms out wide, causing the muscles of his chest and stomach to pull taut. "How am I different?"

Gar bore down hard, grinding his teeth together. "We're different people . . . and I'm not talking physically."

"Neither am I." Faolan didn't move, spread out for inspection. "Question still stands."

Not one to admit when he didn't understand what the hell was going on, Gar rose to his feet, careful not to brush against him. Faolan's long hair kissed the tops of his shoulders, calling out to Gar to touch, grab hold of, tug. Resisting the urge, he circled around behind Faolan's near-naked body, surprised by the amount of body heat coming off his skin.

"Have you figured it out yet?" Faolan spoke with a lover's voice, soft and low.

Gar hadn't. The first touch of his fingers along the muscles of Faolan's back elicited a gasp from him. Holding his position, Faolan allowed the exploration, giving silent permission for Gar to do what he willed.

Four pink nail tracks marred the flawless skin as Gar scratched down to the base of his spine. The answering groan gave him a clue to what Faolan was getting at.

"Skin." Gar kept his voice low, soothing. "Holds everything inside."

Placing both hands on Faolan's hips, he pressed his thumbs into the small of his back.

"Muscles." Underlying strength keeping them moving. Gar knew how hard it was for Faolan to continue on, and felt a small measure of pride that he'd been chosen as Faolan's confidant.

The top of Faolan's pants hung neatly on his hips, held fast by a belt. Gar reached around to fumble with the buckle, needing to feel the heat of Faolan's body completely pressed against his. It didn't feel right having a barrier between them. Not after everything they'd been through.

When had the conversation shifted to seduction in his mind? He couldn't be sure. One more talent Faolan possessed—that of misdirection.

"Clothing?" Faolan offered in an amused tone.

"Mine's better."

"Agreed."

Faolan's pants fell open with the pop of the button, giving Gar the access he wanted. Holding his passions in check, he slid his hand up instead of down, enjoying the quivering muscles beneath his touch. The strength of the other man, a match for Gar in every way.

Gar pressed his mouth to the shoulder before him and whispered against the skin. "Stomach."

Faolan sighed as he leaned back against him. "Yes."

Gar found Faolan's nipples easily, rolling the hard nubs between his forefingers and thumbs. "We both like this."

"Gods damn you."

Gar bit down where he'd kissed a moment earlier. "I'm answering your question."

"Answer faster."

He brushed the pad of his thumb across Faolan's collarbone and up to fill in the hollow of his throat before caressing his Adam's apple.

"Neck."

"Go . . . lower."

"No."

"Gar—"

"*No.*"

Faolan's body started to shake from the strain of holding his arms in place. As much as he enjoyed the tremble, Gar knew there were better things for those talented hands to be doing.

Breathing open-mouthed against Faolan's skin, he shifted his hands so they slid along the top of Faolan's arms to gently pull them down to his sides.

"Touch me."

Faolan's fingers hooked into the top of Gar's pants. He hadn't been able to put on any of his suits, most of his clothing having been ruined along with his ship. Faolan had managed to salvage a few pairs of pants and several shirts, but they were in such poor condition he might as well not have anything at all. So when he jerked Gar's hips hard, tearing at the fabric, Gar hissed.

"If you destroy these, I'll have nothing to wear." *I'll be exposed. The universe will see the man I really am.*

"Leaving you naked? I can live with that."

Gar growled and bit Faolan's shoulder as he grasped his now-straining erection. "You're interrupting."

"Sorry," Faolan said in between pants. "Continue."

"Thank you. I believe I was right about here." Gar squeezed Faolan's firm shaft. "Cock."

Faolan's head fell back, landing on Gar's shoulder. "What does this tell you?"

"It doesn't mean we're the same."

Faolan turned in Gar's arms. Hips and erections pressed together. He reached up and pushed the palm of his hand to Gar's chest. "Heart," he whispered.

The steady rhythm of Gar's heartbeat increased, making it difficult for him to catch his breath. Faolan leaned in and kissed his forehead. "Mind."

"Faolan—"

"Voice." The kiss silenced any further protest.

Gar's growing emotions made it difficult for him to see past why getting closer to the captain was a bad idea. Faolan was the most passionate man he'd ever known. How could he possibly leave him behind when there was so much potential between them?

Tongues clashed, teeth nipped at sensitive flesh, fingers clutched and pressed against heated skin. Gar knew he was sinking into a place he couldn't easily escape. A cosmic force so strong he'd be bound to this ship and the people on board for a very long time.

"Naked," he finally managed after breaking for air. "Now."

The normal cocky grin didn't materialize on Faolan's face. "Only if you promise to stay with me. To give us a chance."

Gar began to shake, and let his gaze fall away. "I don't want anything to happen to you."

"What?" Faolan lifted Gar's chin. "Nothing's going to happen to me. Not because of you at least."

"You don't understand—"

"You're right, I don't. Right now, I don't want you thinking about whatever curse is hanging over your head. In this room, there's just the two of us. Okay?" To reinforce his point, Faolan rolled his hips, grinding their cocks together.

Gar groaned and reached blindly to pull Faolan's pants off. "I think I mentioned naked."

This time there was no protest.

Deft hands made short work of their remaining clothing. Gar let himself be pushed down to the bed, spreading his legs wide to make room for Faolan. His skin tingled as Faolan's gaze traveled the length of his body.

"I'll never get tired of seeing you like this."

"I'm sure you say that to all your lovers." Gar didn't pull away even though he was scared to see the painful truth.

Kneeling between Gar's legs, Faolan looked into his eyes, his sincerity clearly visible. "I may flirt with anything that has a heartbeat, but it doesn't mean I'm not faithful to those who are important to me. I don't sleep around and would never do anything to hurt you."

Gar thought his heart would burst. Swallowing, he did his best to blink back the tears threatening to build in his eyes.

"I believe you," he whispered. Raising his head, he sucked on Faolan's bottom lip. "I believe you."

Faolan slid his arm beneath Gar's head, lifting him to gain better access to his neck. With their bodies fully pressed together, their hips took on a life of their own, canting small thrusts against each other in a bid to gain more friction. Gar gasped at the head-to-toe warmth enveloping him. His body relaxed even as his brain tried to adjust to what was going on.

Faolan moaned. "That feels so good, Gar."

It did—better than anything else he'd ever experienced. Gar wanted more.

Bending his legs so his knees hugged Faolan's sides, he ignored the slight pain in his leg as he tilted his hips and rubbed his balls against Faolan's shaft. "Show me how we're alike."

Faolan stilled. "What?"

A hot flush crept beneath Gar's skin. "Fuck me."

Faolan's eyes rolled shut as a powerful shudder rocked him. "Gods. You're going to kill me."

With the plea out there, Gar couldn't hold back. He grabbed Faolan's hips, pulling him hard against his body. "Please, show me what it's like. I don't want it to be anyone else but you. You wanted me to beg, well, I'm begging. *Please*, Faolan. I want to feel you inside my body. Now."

Letting out a growl, Faolan slid off the berth and to his feet, strode across the floor to a small drawer, and jerked it open. Confused, Gar was about to ask what he'd done wrong when Faolan turned, holding an object up for his inspection.

"I'm going to make this so good for you, you won't dream of taking another lover for the rest of your life."

If his heart had been beating fast before, now it was an outright gallop. "Don't take too long or I might change my mind."

Faolan licked his lips. "Don't even think of leaving. Not until I've fucked you senseless."

"Better hurry up and stop me, then."

Rather than climb back on top of him, Faolan dropped to the side of the bed between Gar's thighs. Hooking his arms beneath Gar's knees, he yanked him forward until his ass was flush with the edge of the bed. Heat from Faolan's breath teased the sensitive flesh of his engorged cock, sending shivers and gooseflesh exploding across his skin. "First things first."

Gar arched off the bed as Faolan took the tip of his cock into his mouth, swirling his tongue around the sensitive crown before sucking hard. Gar groaned, hands flying to Faolan's head. He threaded his fingers through the silken strands of his hair.

"So good." He turned his head and buried his face in the sheets. The combined scent of Faolan and himself assaulted his senses, dragging another moan from his chest as Faolan took him all the way down his throat.

Muscles contracted around Gar's shaft, then the scrape of teeth as Faolan slowly pulled himself off. "Best thing I've had to eat in days."

Gar fought against the chuckle, but lost. "I don't believe you."

"This is meant to be enjoyed, savored like the best alcohol or finest food. It doesn't have to be serious to be any less meaningful." Before Gar could respond, Faolan lowered his head and sucked Gar's balls into his mouth.

Quick flicks of Faolan's tongue launched Gar high into the realm of pleasure. Any last remnants of loneliness he'd felt were chased away by the care with which Faolan was loving him. So distracted by Faolan's wicked mouth and his own torrent of emotions, he didn't notice the lube-coated finger pushing into his ass until the tip breached the tight ring of muscles.

On instinct, his body tensed against the intrusion, bucking away. Faolan was ready for the reaction and pushed Gar's hips back down, keeping him in place. Faolan didn't move his hand as he returned his attention to licking a stripe along the length of Gar's cock.

Slowly, the tension melted into pleasure as Faolan's mouth worked on Gar's shaft, the stubble from his chin scraping the skin as he went. Gar had almost forgotten about Faolan's hand until he started pumping his finger in and out of Gar's ass in a counter-rhythm to his mouth. Gar inhaled sharply through his nose and opened his legs wider when Faolan brushed against his prostate.

"Fuck." He wanted to cry from the perfection of it all. "More."

Faolan hummed and added a second finger. The burn increased as Gar's muscles widened under Faolan's ministrations. Higher and higher he climbed until his body was so taut he thought he'd snap in two.

"Please, please, let me come." Gar tugged at the head between his legs. "Please."

Faolan pulled off him with a pop and slowly inched his fingers from Gar's ass. "No. I want to be buried deep inside you when you do. I want to feel every inch of your body squeeze around me when you finally lose control." Hooking a hand under each knee, he pushed Gar back until they were in the center of the bed, then lifted his legs until his ass rested on Faolan's thighs. It was then Faolan leaned over to place a kiss on Gar's chin. "I want to look in your eyes when you come, so you know it was me who brought you there."

Gar caressed Faolan's face and smiled. "Like I could forget it was you."

Still . . . he knew the bliss of taking another person, of being completely surrounded and milked to completion. Being in the opposite position was foreign and more than a little terrifying.

Faolan shifted back, covered his hand with more lube, and stroked his cock, coating it completely. "Relax. If you tense up, this won't be as good."

"I'm not a virgin." Gar rolled his eyes while convincing his body this really would be good. He could trust Faolan like no other person.

"You are like this. But not for much longer."

Faolan bent his head and distracted him with a long, lazy kiss. The almost languid pace did the trick as the tension left Gar's body and the blood surged once more to his shaft. The pressure from Faolan's cock as he pressed in wasn't as bad as Gar had anticipated. Neither was the slow burn of muscles stretching to accommodate his girth. Faolan didn't stop, simply kept pushing forward and kissing Gar senseless. He didn't realize when Faolan bottomed out, his balls flush against Gar's ass.

They stayed that way for a minute. Faolan bumped his nose along Gar's jaw, licking at the skin of his neck, cooing soft nonsense words while Gar's body adjusted. It was overwhelming, being this close to another person. The same as topping, yet completely different. Instead of the fear he thought he'd feel, he was able to let go. Faolan would be there to catch him if anything went wrong.

Someone was there to look after him.

"I'm okay." He nipped at Faolan's earlobe. "And you made a promise."

"Good, because I'm going to fuck you now." Faolan kissed along Gar's jawline. "Going to show you heaven."

Pulling out until the tip of his cock remained barely sheathed, Faolan pushed back in with one smooth stroke. There was pain, but less than before. After several repeated thrusts, Gar's body relaxed, allowed Faolan to go deep. He groaned and clutched Faolan's shoulders, praying he could hold it together long enough to enjoy this ride to its fullest.

They set a fast pace, Faolan's hips snapping forward while Gar lifted his ass to meet him. His thoughts deserted him, leaving him only able to feel as his body came alive under Faolan's touch.

"So close, Gar." Faolan's face tightened in concentration. "Can't wait much longer. Want you to come first."

Long fingers wrapped around Gar's cock, Faolan stroked him with a firm, steady beat. Coupled with the constant attack against his prostate, he couldn't hold back. Bunching the sheets in his fists, he arched his back off the bed and came hard. Cum shot over Faolan's hand to cover both their stomachs. Only once he opened his eyes again did Faolan release his cock.

"Perfect," Faolan said softly.

Yes, Gar was beginning to see they were.

He lightly bit Faolan's chin. "You now."

Angling his hips even more, he clamped down on Faolan's cock until Faolan's mouth made a perfect *O* and he cried out, pumping mercilessly into Gar's eager body. Liquid heat flooded him, and Gar clung to the sensations. Faolan had given him everything—everything Gar was comfortable asking for. Finally, *blessedly*, Faolan collapsed on top of him.

Their competing harsh breaths were the only sounds filling the room for a long time. An ache in his ass compelled Gar to shift onto his side, facing Faolan, who lay on his back. Without opening his eyes, Faolan tossed an arm across Gar's shoulders to pull him flush against his body.

It felt right, the closeness they shared alone in the dark of their bedroom.

Gar drew circles on Faolan's chest. "I think I understand now."

A kiss to his temple. "Good."

How much time had passed as they were lying in each other's arms, he wasn't sure. He must have drifted off and been asleep for some time, as the sweat on his skin had already dried and cooled when he was startled awake.

Something wasn't right. A beep from the com system caught his attention and brought a groan from Faolan. "Can't they leave us alone for five minutes?"

"Been longer than that. Let me answer it."

"Mmm, 'kay."

Gar smiled and placed a kiss to Faolan's chest before getting up and finding his pants to answer the com. When Mace's face appeared, he was eternally thankful he'd dressed as much as he had.

Mace groaned and covered her eyes with her hand. "Do you have to answer the com naked? Dear gods!"

"I was sleeping." Not a complete lie. "What can I do for you, Macie?"

The traces of humor on her face mere seconds ago dropped off as she sighed. "We have a problem."

Of course they did. "Not more Loyalists, I hope."

"No, that would be easy in comparison. We intercepted a transmission a few moments ago."

Gar cocked an eyebrow. "And?"

"Krieg knows you're alive and with us. They've put a bounty on your head."

CHAPTER

FIFTEEN

"This guy is really pissing me off." Faolan scanned the intercepted message, his anger rising with each passing moment. "Are you sure you have no idea why Krieg would want you dead?"

Gar didn't move, but Faolan could feel the tension coming off him in waves. "Everything was fine last time I saw him."

"He just gave you your assignment like normal?"

"Other than he wanted me to get you. Been a while since I've had to do a pickup. He usually keeps me for more delicate situations."

The more Faolan thought on the situation, the less it made sense. "Somehow Jason knew I was going to be on Tybal even before he sent you."

"Not possible." Gar leaned forward, bracing one hand on the back of Faolan's chair and the other on the computer console. With their bodies so close, it took all of Faolan's willpower not to lean back and make contact. He didn't think Mace would appreciate seeing her newly rediscovered brother get publicly fondled. Gar kept talking, seemingly oblivious to Faolan's struggle. "I was there when the call came in about your presence, which in itself is a bit out of the ordinary. It's been nearly a year since I'd set down on one of his bases. He was definitely surprised you'd turned up on his doorstep, almost as much as when I docked with his ship."

Mace made a disgusted sound. "I know you're a pain in the ass, Faolan, but I can't believe Jason would think you could corrupt Gar over your mind-reading thing." She bumped her shoulder into Gar. "Corrupt you with other things—"

"Okay, thanks for that." Gar straightened. "Jason always kept me closer than the others. I assumed it was because he'd saved my ass on Zeten. Maybe it was more than that."

Faolan didn't like where this was going. "You don't think it's a coincidence I found Mace and Krieg found you."

Gar held his gaze, and Faolan could see the pain of betrayal clear in his eyes. "It would make sense if Jason knew you'd left with Mace. He may have had a reason for keeping us apart or at least not wanting me to find out something you knew."

"Easier to kill us both than to deal with the situation."

"It also explains why my intel wasn't clear on your location and I was forced to spend more time looking for you than normal. Jason was buying time to get the tracker installed on my ship. Bastard!" Gar picked up the datapad from the table and threw it against the wall.

"*Damn it*, Gar!" Mace jumped back, narrowly avoiding bits of glass and plastic as it smashed apart.

On his feet in a heartbeat, Faolan stepped between the siblings, catching Mace by the shoulders. "We need to go after this asshole and put him down. I don't care if he's the head of the guild or not."

Mace continued to glare at Gar, her face flushed with anger. "It's going to take a small army to go after someone as well-protected as Krieg. Seeing as he knows Gar is alive, he'll be ready for an attack."

"Then we'll have to be even more ready. I want you to call in some favors, get us a makeshift pirate army and we'll take this guy out. There aren't many in the sector who will be upset by the fact, either."

"No."

They both turned to look at Gar. Faolan wanted to protest, but Mace beat him to it. "What the hell do you mean, *no*? Jason tried to kill you and Faolan. You've got a bounty on your head bigger than Faolan's, for gods' sake. You can't let this go."

Gar tugged at the bottom of his one remaining suit jacket, his knuckles white from the tension. "No one is going after him but me."

A knot of tension coiled in Faolan's stomach. "Mace, mind giving us a minute?"

"Faolan, I really think—"

"Please." He knew she'd realize it wasn't a request.

Nodding, she stepped away from Faolan. "Let me know what you need done, Captain."

He hated cutting Mace out of this, but she wasn't thinking clearly when it came to her brother. He could claim the same impairment, but would never admit it out loud. Besides, if she caught wind of what he was about to propose, Mace would either lock them both in the brig or try to come along—neither of which were acceptable options. One of them had to survive.

"I won't risk anyone else's life over this mess, Faolan. There's nothing you can say to change my mind."

"I'm going with you."

Gar's mouth fell open, his protest dead in the air. "What?"

Faolan shrugged. "If you don't want to go in guns blazing, I'm fine with that. Sneak attack through the back door, good enough. But if you think for even a second I'm going to let you go in alone, you're insane."

"I'm not going to risk your life." Gar stepped up and caressed Faolan's cheek. "Don't ask me to do that."

It would have been a sweet sentiment if he wasn't living under a death sentence anyway. "If I have the choice between dying now to help you avenge yourself, or a year from now regretting the fact I didn't, I know which one I'll take."

Gar stepped away, shaking his head and squeezing the back of his neck with his hand. "You have Mace to look after, and your ship."

"They'll learn to get by without me." Sooner or later that was an inescapable truth. "Mace is a tough girl, she'll be fine. I trust her to run things once I'm gone."

"Gods, Faolan." Gar crossed his arms. "You didn't even know me a few weeks ago. Why are you doing this?"

It had taken him a while, but Faolan now knew most of Gar's tells. The way his brow pulled tight, the deep lines of his frown, the lost-boy look in his eyes: they all told him how scared and confused Gar really was.

Faolan closed the distance between them, cupped Gar's face in his hands, and kissed him hard. He infused it with everything he felt for the man, some of which he didn't have the heart to voice yet. He wanted the life he knew he could give Gar. A normal life on some backwater planet where they could settle down and have some fun. He brought to mind every dream and desire he had and willed Gar to feel the same. The kiss deepened as Gar explored his mouth and hugged him in a firm embrace. The concealed blades hidden beneath

Gar's jacket dug into Faolan's side. Danger and passion, all in one man. How could he resist?

The kiss slowed, and he pulled back enough to run his hand along Gar's forearm. He hummed pleasantly in his throat as he thumbed the blade guard.

"I want to see these in action," he said softly against Gar's lips. "Want to see what you can do."

"Trying to sweet-talk me won't work, Wolf." Gar smiled before he nipped at Faolan's chin. "I can't talk you out of this, can I?"

"Nope."

"Should I even bother trying?"

"Waste of time. We should start planning instead."

"You know anything we try will most likely get us killed." Gar cocked an eyebrow.

"Kill or be killed. Jason won't back down now. You know it as well as I do." Faolan ran his thumb along Gar's cheekbone. "At least this way you can try to get some answers."

"I'll get them all right. Jason may think he'll be able to keep me out, but I'll get him."

One last quick kiss and Faolan stepped away. "We'll get the bastard together. Just need a good plan."

Gar chuckled. "And a ship. As nice as she is, the *Belle Kurve* is a bit on the obvious side and clearly the *Geilt* is in no shape to go anywhere."

"I have an idea of where we can get one, but we'll have to move quickly."

He sat in front of his computer, knowing exactly who could help them out. "I have an acquaintance in this sector who owes me for getting him out of a scrape a few years back. He's been waiting for me to collect."

"What about Mace?" Gar moved closer, but stayed out of sight of the com display. "I don't want her involved."

"The easiest way to keep her safe is to keep her in the loop. Include her, or else she'll show up when you least want her to."

"Speaking from experience?"

"Little shit got herself knee-deep into trouble once, it took me a laser blaster and a— Styles, my friend!"

The hunch-shouldered man straightened as much as he ever did. Faolan didn't trust him very far, but knew he wouldn't go back against a debt owed. Pirate's code and all that.

"Wolf. You're not dead yet?"

Faolan grinned and winked. "Not from lack of trying. I've come to collect."

"I figured this wasn't a social call. What do you need?"

"A ship, small. No bigger than a cruiser, with lots of guns."

Gar leaned close so he could whisper, "Shields."

"Shields too if you have them." Faolan half turned to smirk at Gar. "Anything else, darling?"

Gar rolled his eyes. "Ass."

Styles made a clucking noise, garnering Faolan's attention. "New girlfriend?"

All expression dropped from Gar's face as he moved into the com's view. The change in Styles was nearly comical when he realized who was with Faolan.

"I kn-know you." The small man visibly shrank on the screen. "You're that bounty hunter."

"The ship better be top of the line." Gar raised a single eyebrow. "I'd hate to be disappointed."

"You bastard, Wolf." Styles sneered. "When and where?"

"Now and the Orin cluster."

"Am I getting it back?"

Faolan kept his smile in place, but his expression hardened. He knew the effect it would have on Styles and wasn't disappointed. "Consider it paying your debt in full."

Styles muttered something in his native language before clucking his tongue again. "Fine. I can get you one within three hours."

"Perfect! Always a pleasure doing business with you." Faolan didn't wait for the response and closed the com.

"Do you trust him?" Gar relaxed, leaning against the side of his chair.

"Not particularly. I do trust he's scared enough of Mace not to kill me or else she'll tear him apart."

"Lovely creature, my sister."

"Speaking of whom, let's get the *Belle Kurve* in position and give Mace something to do."

Faolan stood and silently enjoyed the way Gar fell into step behind him as they walked. It felt right, this unexpected companionship—too bad they were both heading toward a messy death.

Attachments always made situations like these hard to handle. It simply wasn't fair that Gar and Mace had found each other, only to have Jason threaten their lives. Faolan wanted to give them both the chance to get to know each other. Given the opportunity, he would sacrifice himself and save Gar.

"Mace! We have a plan." He made sure he sounded extra confident as they entered the cockpit and hoped she would actually believe him for once.

Hands on her hips, she glared at him. "Does it involve me?"

"Of course, pet. Wouldn't dream of leaving you out."

Gar let out a soft snort behind him. Mace heard it too and pointed a finger at him. "Shut it."

Faolan pretended to ignore the interruption. "Gar and I have a ship and are going to hit Jason deep in his own house."

"Doesn't sound like I'm a part of this so far."

As usual, he hadn't thought the entire thing out before talking. With Mace, he often found it better to simply take things off the cuff. Before he answered, Gar spoke up.

"We need you to call in all those favors Faolan mentioned. Get as many ships together as you can and have them gather near a major dimension gate."

Mace frowned. "Why?"

"Because Jason wouldn't expect us to come in alone. He'll be looking for a group of pirate ships."

Gods, he was a smart one. Faolan grinned and ran his hand down the length of Gar's back. "We're going to give him what he expects."

"And hit him in a way he doesn't. Very nice, big brother." Mace smiled, punching Gar in the shoulder. "You're not too bad."

Gar rolled his eyes. "You can compliment me when we come back in one piece."

Clapping his hands together, Faolan enjoyed the rush of excitement. "Let's get to work."

The ship wasn't exactly what Faolan had in mind. Designed for a race he was convinced had tentacles instead of two arms, the cockpit was crowded and hot, even with only the two of them. One look inside had the added bonus of cementing Mace's role of staying on the *Belle Kurve* to run operations there.

"Entering the planet's atmosphere." Gar's voice was a calming presence in the riot of lights, sensors, and alarms.

"I can't believe Jason runs the guild from Zeten." Ballsy didn't begin to describe the move. "You'd think the high level of crime and Loyalist activity would keep him far away from here."

Gar shrugged and hit the cloaking sensors. "He plays both sides pretty close. Has for years. I think he gets a rush thinking he's untouchable."

"Not for much longer." Faolan squeezed Gar's shoulder. "We'll put this right."

"Damn straight we will."

They'd spoken very little since departing from the *Belle Kurve*. Gar's mood had darkened noticeably the closer they got to his home. Faolan didn't need to read Gar's mind to know ghosts from the past had come screaming to the present. The weight of the silence had given Faolan more time than he normally preferred to think on his own condition.

The meds weren't doing what he needed them to. Before leaving, he'd injected himself with another dose, not wanting to risk a relapse in the middle of a firefight. Still, the concerns and the nature of his declining state were staring him in the face. Even if by some small miracle he survived this little adventure with Gar, his life was rapidly coming to an end.

"You know . . ." Gar started before turning away to intently study a reading on the screen.

When he didn't continue, Faolan faced him. "You know . . . what?"

Gar blushed as he shrugged. "I met you once before. Years ago."

"Really?" Faolan knew he would have recalled Gar. There was very little he could have done to hide his natural appeal. "I don't remember."

"You wouldn't have. I was only a kid, sixteen. I was following around one of the more experienced bounty hunters, learning the ropes. He'd cornered you in a bar on Prymax. You managed to talk your way to the back alley and then tricked him into letting you go. I was . . . impressed."

Faolan had a vague recollection of the event. "I live to be burned into the minds of the people I've scammed." He winked at Gar.

"It was one of the reasons I wasn't too upset when Jason gave me this assignment. I wanted to see you again."

Faolan caught Gar looking at him from the corner of his eye, reached out and squeezed his hand. "I'm glad you did."

The ship chose that moment to shudder violently. "Is that cloak going to hold through the atmospheric descent?" Despite the prospect of a painful future death, he didn't want to blow up because of a substandard part. "Just because Styles came through for us with the ship, it doesn't mean I trust the quality."

Gar snorted, but checked the scanner anyway. "It's holding. We'll be through the sensor hole in fifteen minutes. Then we can touch down in a safe spot I know and slip into the guild headquarters. At least Jason sent the bulk of his fleet off to chase Mace and her army. We won't have to defend ourselves as much."

"Sounds good." Despite having all the time in the world to think about how to phrase this, Faolan still wasn't sure. *Nothing for it.* "I have a favor to ask."

"Hmm?"

Reaching into his pocket, Faolan snagged the stone and pulled it out. "I want you to wear this when we're down there."

Gar's eyes grew impossibly wide, but he made no move to take the chain. "Why?"

"It worked better for you than anyone else who's tried it. I figure you know Jason. This confrontation might have him thinking thoughts he'd never verbalize. Might get you the answers you want faster."

"What about you? Selling it to get what you need?" Gar shook his head and turned forward. "I'm not going to risk losing it."

"You know as well as I do the chances of us getting out of here alive are close to zero. At least this way you can die with a clear understanding of what happened." Not giving Gar the option of protesting any further, Faolan slipped the chain over his head. "Keep it under your shirt and no one will know."

"Faolan—"

"We've broken through." He sat back down in his seat and immediately focused on the computer. "Set the approach vector now." The pause was followed by a sigh and the rustle of clothing, making him smile.

"In and locked. Be ready to move the second we touch down."

"I'll follow your lead."

The ship rattled from the strong easterly wind whipping at them as they descended, making conversation impossible. It had been a long time since Faolan had participated in a raid like this. Good for a change.

They remained undetected as Gar set them down in a valley with heavy vegetation. Faolan had spotted several large buildings on the outskirts of the city and could only assume this was the location of the infamous guild. "How long will it take us to hike there?"

"Normally I'd say not long, but seeing as we need to avoid the guards, I'm not sure."

"We better move it, then."

Night was falling, long shadows making it easier for them to cover most of the distance unnoticed. Faolan was impressed at the ease with which Gar moved, even wearing the heavy overcoat and full suit they'd managed to salvage from the *Geilt*.

His limbs felt numb the longer they traipsed up the rocky terrain toward their target. He knew Gar was keeping an eye on him, slowing his pace when he fell too far behind. Thankfully, he never verbalized his concerns, and kept moving forward. One quick dash from the tree line to a building on the outer edge of the city, and they were finally safe.

As safe as they could be walking into the heart of enemy territory.

Gar stepped close beside him as they walked, heads down and eyes averted from any passersby. "Jason's headquarters are in a building not far from here, but toward the center of town."

"Going in through a crowd of civilians. Fun." Faolan sighed and shifted closer. "So how do you want to do this? Sneak in the back door?"

Gar stopped moving, shoving his hands in his pockets. "Nope, going to use a different approach."

Faolan really didn't like the sound of this. "What do you have planned? Not something stupid, is it?"

Crooking his finger at Faolan to follow, Gar strode off straight into the middle of town. He made no move to mask his appearance nor hide his intent from anyone in sight. Groaning, Faolan took off after him.

Gar stopped alongside a statue, presumably of a Zeten war hero. He didn't move—there was no scanning the crowds, secret codes, nothing. Faolan slowed his pace and sauntered over to his side as casually as he could manage.

"This doesn't seem like a smart plan, Stitt."

"The easiest way to see Jason is to let him know I'm here. He'll send someone to collect us shortly."

True enough, it only took a few minutes for three large men, clearly some of the less elegant of the bounty hunters Jason had on staff, to materialize before them. Gar gave no visual response or indication of any nervousness. The trio sneered down at them, and Faolan couldn't help but chuckle.

"Stitt." The largest of the three nodded at Gar. "You've got balls."

"Take us to Jason."

The man laughed, causing several onlookers to scurry away. "Fuck you. You're not leaving this place—"

Gar stepped forward, blade springing from his hidden sheath. "Let me rephrase. Jason is expecting me."

Faolan moved one hand to his sword hilt and the other to the butt of his blaster. If they were heading for a fight, he wanted to be ready. The trio remained still until the one in the rear pressed his finger to his ear.

"Yes, sir."

Gar stiffened but didn't remove his blade from the big man's throat.

The hunter with the earpiece coughed and stepped away from his partners. "Jason said to bring you to him. He also asked that you don't kill the help."

Gar's lips twitched into a smile. "No promises. Gentlemen, lead the way."

Faolan fell into step by Gar's side, not surprised to note two additional men joining them to bring up the rear of the group. Things were going to get messy.

CHAPTER
SIXTEEN

I *hope you know what you're doing, Gar.*

He fought the urge to snort at Faolan's thoughts. Gar liked to think he knew his former boss very well. He knew that given a slightly different set of circumstances, it would be someone like himself bringing in the marks, and not some low-level hunters who hadn't earned the right to leave the guild's home territory yet. Still, he should be thankful the men weren't as experienced as they could be.

Once we kick their asses, I'm going to take you out for a meal. You're too skinny.

Gar snapped his head to look at Faolan. The stupid ass should know better than to flirt in a situation like this.

Don't stare at me or they'll think something's up.

Turning to look at the back of the largest bounty hunter, Gar let out a short huff to express his discontent.

Stuff it, Stitt. If I'm going to die, I'm damn well going to enjoy myself.

The main entrance to the guild wasn't what most people expected. The small metal door bore no decoration, and it was pitted on the outside from the hail and flying rocks frequently kicked up in the planet's notorious windstorms. There was no visible high-level security, nor were there any armed guards posted. Anyone could walk into the heart of the building and talk to those inside.

Getting out was what proved difficult for most.

The leader of the hunter trio banged on the door three times before pressing the release and ushering them in. Gar was temporarily blinded as his eyes adjusted to the sudden darkness. It didn't stop him from moving forward, knowing the route from years of walking it.

He felt more than heard Faolan stumble; reaching out, Gar grabbed his forearm to lead him the right way.

Don't let me run into any walls. Be a shame to mark up my pretty face.

Gar squeezed his arm and tugged hard.

"Jason is in his office." The leader's voice was muffled by the narrow hall. "I trust you know the way."

"Been there a few times." Gar pushed past the men, dragging Faolan with him. "I suggest you men go into hiding. You won't want to get caught in the crossfire."

His eyes had adjusted enough for Gar to see the other hunter's sneer. "Yeah right, asshole."

Faolan chuckled. "I'll enjoy watching him kick your ass later. Been fun, boys."

Each step Gar took brought his anger a bit closer to the surface. He'd given everything to this place. Done things bordering on the unacceptable, walked a tight line between what needed to be done and what his conscience could allow. The more he thought on it, the more he realized how much of himself he'd sacrificed to become a man he really didn't like.

Jason had done this to him, pushing him when he tried to walk away or back down. Jason had been the one who told him his life would be forfeit if he tried to leave the guild. Yet Jason was the one who betrayed him in the end. Gar wanted payback.

I can feel you seething from here, Gar. Keep a calm head or else they've won before we've started.

Gar almost stopped to yell at Faolan to stay out of his mind when he realized it was the other way around. How Faolan had grown to know him as well as he did in such a short period of time was a mystery, and it scared him.

Turning the corner once, then again, brought them within short distance from Jason's office. Gar knew the guild's leader would be more than ready for them—guns, lasers, and gas were all possible. *Probably all three.* He'd have to stay sharp if he was going to pull off his plan and get Faolan out in one piece.

They paused before entering the room, and Faolan's hand found his for a quick squeeze. *We'll blast this fucker and be home for breakfast.*

Gar allowed himself a moment to savor the contact. "Here's hoping."

Taking a deep breath, he released Faolan's hand and marched inside. Sitting behind the desk, hands folded neatly in front of him, sat the focus of his wrath. Gar stopped a few feet away, laced his fingers behind his back and stared at his surrogate father.

"Krieg." Gar nodded.

Shit, you had a picture of him on the Geilt. *I saw it in your quarters.*

"Stitt. I see you finally brought your mark in." Jason's gaze never left his, nor did he acknowledge Faolan in any way.

The gray in his hair looked more pronounced than Gar had ever remembered seeing it before. Whether it was due to a sudden rush of stress or simply him seeing Jason in a new light, it didn't matter. Jason had betrayed him.

"Faolan came with me." His voice remained calm and even, despite his surging anger. "And we'll be leaving together."

Focus on his thoughts, Faolan's voice prodded in his mind.

Lifting his chin, Gar focused his attention solely on Jason, attempting to block out everything else. Jason shook his head and tsked as he pressed the not-so-secret button beneath his desk. The door behind them slid shut, locking them in.

"Interesting place you have here, Jason. You don't mind if I call you Jason, do you?" Faolan sauntered to Gar's side, thumbs hooked in the tops of his pants. "Can't say I'm impressed with the welcome, though. Might want to do some hospitality training with your staff. I mean really, how hard is it to have them offer us a drink or something to eat? Very rude."

Leaning back in his seat, Jason steepled his hands together and let his gaze finally move to Faolan. "Nice to finally meet the infamous Captain Wolf. I'm looking forward to collecting the bounty on your head."

Faolan grinned. "Gar said it was two million. I almost turned myself in. Think of the shit I can buy with that much."

"That's for bringing you in alive. Dead, it's much more."

Turning to slap Gar on the shoulder, Faolan rolled his eyes. "You were holding out on me." *Concentrate on him, Gar. Try to get into his head.*

Gar released a breath and let the tension bleed from his body. He cleared his mind of everything and listened for the soft buzzing he'd felt when he'd first connected to Faolan.

"Gar was always too soft for his own good. It was his biggest shortcoming. One I tried to burn out of him for years."

The first tremor of Jason's mind brushing against his nearly turned Gar's stomach. Where Faolan's thoughts had been warmth and a bright touch, Jason's sent a chill through his soul.

Stupid brat. Will enjoy making him suffer.

The venom behind the thought nearly sent him staggering. Gar squeezed his hands together and let the pain help him focus on the task at hand.

Lifting his chin, he stared his former mentor down. "Enough of this shit, Jason. Why did you want me killed?"

He can't know the truth. "It was clear you weren't living up to your end of the bargain, Stitt." Jason narrowed his gaze, focusing his cold eyes on Gar. "You've been around here long enough to know the penalty for betrayal is death."

"I followed your orders to the letter. I was on my way to get the stone for you." His throat tightened and his body shook from the strain of holding his temper in check. "You sent ships to blow me out of space!"

Was my best chance. Finally clean up this mess. "It was necessary," Jason said with finality.

"Did you even want the bloody thing?" Gar's head couldn't keep up with the barrage of thoughts flying through it. It became difficult to know whose mind was whose.

"Of course I wanted it." *The stone can't be real. Wolf was bluffing.* "But not at the risk of your betrayal." *He'd kill me.* "I'd rather it be blown to space dust than to let you or that pirate use it against me."

Faolan stepped between Gar and Jason, his hand on the hilt of his sword. "And why is that? What were you trying to keep him from learning?"

"Why would you assume I was keeping something from him?" *Gods, they fucking know. Gar must know!*

Gar moved toward Jason without thinking. "Know what?" Faolan's hand on his chest stopped him from closing the distance so he could wrap his hands around Jason's neck. "Tell me!"

Jason's eyes widened, and he dropped his hands to his lap. "What?" *No, he couldn't realize. I made sure he never connected me to their deaths.*

"You killed them." Gar's voice shook as he squeezed Faolan's forearm. "My parents."

Sliced her throat to get him to talk. Framed him for her death. Jason's smile twisted into a scowl. "It was so easy to manipulate you, the other guards. All I had to do was sit in the background and let it all play out."

The universe around Gar paused before everything slotted into place. "No," he whispered.

"You're just like your father—too proud for your own good. He agreed to steal something for me and then tried to go back on the deal. I thought by killing his wife I'd convince him to give in. Fucker wouldn't." *Felt good, blade going in. She cried and cried and pleaded.*

"Gar." Faolan's presence calmed him. "Keep it together."

It was enough reassurance to bring him back to their purpose. Swallowing, he squeezed Faolan's hand in reassurance and stepped forward. "You killed my mother."

"Even that wasn't enough to convince him. You want to blame anyone, blame him."

"What was it you wanted so badly that you were willing to tear my life apart?"

Power. "Stupid ass hid the codes somewhere in his belongings. I've tried to find it," Jason said with a sneer. "No luck." *Needed the key to control everything.*

The stopwatch. Gar remembered the day his dad had handed it over to him. Telling him how special it was and to keep it safe. It was the one item he'd kept on his person most days when he was younger. Jason wouldn't have known. If the codes were anywhere, it was there.

"Fucker." Gar's world spun around him, full of confusion.

"Your father was just as shortsighted as you. I couldn't expect someone like you to understand, Stitt." *Bastard betrayed me, like his kid.*

"Why don't you explain it to me, then?" Faolan slowly pulled his sword from the sheath, tip pointed at the floor.

Jason's gaze flicked between them. "You think I'm scared of a sword? I'm well aware of Gar and his knives. Don't you think I prepared for that?" *Personal shield will fry them.*

Gar's hand stopped Faolan from moving too close. "He has an electro shield."

"How did you . . .?" *Gods, it's like he's reading my mind. Is the stone real?*

"Answer the question, Jason." Gar reached into his coat and thumbed the shock charge.

"Fine, you want to know?" Jason shoved his chair back and yanked out the blaster he had beneath the desk. "You were there with me when Wolf here showed up on Tybal. There was no one else around, so I had to send you, else it would have looked suspicious. I couldn't take the chance you'd figure things out once you spent time with Wolf, so I put a bounty on your head. Figured it was about time I cleaned up that mess from ten years ago."

"Wait a minute." Faolan frowned, concentrating on Jason. "I *know* you."

Gar didn't want to risk taking his eyes off Jason. "Faolan?"

"The reason Kayla and I were on Zeten ten years ago, the medical scam. Jason here was the bastard we cleaned out."

Jason powered up the blaster to full and leaned forward, pointing the barrel square at Faolan's chest. "It was a distraction I couldn't afford. Don't worry though, I got even." *Killed him in the end. Slow and painful.*

Faolan frowned. "What?"

Gods. Gar shook his head. "The poison. That was you?"

"Had a friend who owed me a favor. When he told me you'd shown up, I got him to give you a little extra something for me. How are you feeling these days, Wolf? Headaches and weakness kicked in yet? Vomiting blood?"

"Shit." Faolan's voice had lost all sense of bravado.

"You'd caused me to lose track of Gar's father, at least until little Gar was ever so helpful and led me straight to him. Figured the punishment was fitting."

Pain and guilt made Gar sick, but not as much as the pure menace rolling through Jason's mind.

Never got the codes. "I held your mom hostage, Stitt, as incentive to convince your father to steal the Loyalist codes to their computer mainframe. He was the only one on the colony who had access. With those I could have hacked in and controlled everything from the supply chain to the flow of currency."

"He didn't give them to you." Respect for his dad increased tenfold. "Why keep me around? Why not kill me like you did my parents and sister?" The last thing he wanted was to let Jason know Mace still lived. She could hide forever, safe on the *Belle Kurve*.

"I knew your father gave you the codes. Thought if I kept you around long enough you'd let the location slip." *Wanted to make you suffer.* "I could use them to learn their programming safeguards. Still hack in."

"But if I put two and two together and realized you were the man from Zeten I'd scammed, I might put Gar on the path to learning you butchered his family." Faolan's voice dropped to a harsh whisper. "You bastard." *He needs to pay.*

It took Gar a second to realize what Faolan was planning, too long to react. Faolan shoved him hard to the side as Jason fired the blaster. The beam exploded on the floor in the space where he'd been moments ago. Gar managed to roll away, avoiding the second blast, and pulled his guns from their holsters. "Faolan!"

Jason twisted his weapon around, shot going wide as Faolan swung his sword in a wide arc. The blast bounced off the wall, to be absorbed by the chair in the far corner. It would only be a matter of seconds before the room was flooded with bounty hunters set on killing them. Gar grabbed the control pad from his pocket and pressed the jammer he'd set before leaving the ship. The room locked down—doors and escape panels frozen shut. No one was getting in or out of the room.

Keep him safe.

Spinning around, Gar looked in time to see Faolan lunge for Jason. "Faolan, no!"

The blade connected with the shield. Screaming, Faolan forced the sword forward until the system overloaded and the metal pierced the wrist strap controlling the shield. The resulting explosion threw Faolan across the room and blinded Gar.

Jason's panicked screams howled through Gar's mind for a terrifying moment before fading to nothingness. Gar pressed his hands to his temples, blinking madly against the pain.

"Jason?"

He was dead.

Scrambling, but failing to get to his feet, Gar crawled across the floor to where Faolan lay unmoving. Pounding on the door from the hall told him that potential exit was blocked by hunters who would cut them to shreds before they ever left the room. It didn't matter. Not if Faolan was hurt. Gar had to help him, somehow save him from this mess.

Gar's hands connected with wetness as he rolled Faolan onto his back. Blood oozed from a cut on Faolan's cheek and a large bruise was already forming on his forehead. Blinking back the sudden rush of tears, Gar wiped the blood away as best he could with his hand shaking. He couldn't lose Faolan. Not yet.

"Faolan? Come on, you bastard, open your eyes." Leaning forward, Gar kissed his cheek and felt for the soft in-out of breath. "Don't do this to me."

Scared. "Ouch," Faolan whispered, so softly Gar almost didn't hear him.

"I'm here. You're okay."

Hurts.

"I know it does. I'm going to get you out of here."

Go.

"Will you shut the hell up and open your eyes. Now, Wolf. Faolan!"

It must have been enough to reach through the concussed fog of Faolan's brain. His eyes were hazy and didn't stay focused for long, but Gar figured it was better than nothing. "Can you stand?"

No. "Yes."

Ignoring his doubt, Gar hauled him to his feet, waiting long enough for him to steady. "We have one shot of getting out of here. Jason always builds in a hidden passage in the event he gets raided. There are only a few of us who know about it and most of them are off planet at the moment."

"Weapons?"

Gar pulled the stunner from his pocket. "I have this and my blaster. Blades are out of the question given your current state."

"Better move." Faolan swayed heavily against him. "Leave me if you have to."

"Will you shut up? On our way we're making a pit stop."

Faolan looked up at him and blinked. Smiling, Gar looped his arm under Faolan's and led him to the wall. "If Jason was the one who poisoned you, then I bet there is something to cure it in the med bay."

"No time."

"It's on our way. Now move, Wolf, before I'm tempted to collect the bounty on your ass."

Without knowing who was present at the base, this would either be an extremely easy exit or immediate death. The passageway was thankfully clear as they moved inside. It took longer than Gar would have liked due to Faolan's condition, but they eventually made it to the med bay's secret door.

Two hunters and one doctor were present, each with weapons pointed toward the main door. They never heard the secret panel slide open or saw the stunner as Gar tossed it into the room. The blinding light and high-pitched blast knocked the three to the ground.

Gar propped Faolan against the wall. "Stay here."

"Like I could go anywhere."

Each second he took to look was a moment less they would have to get out in one piece. Tearing apart the cabinet, he growled in frustration when he realized he didn't have a clue what he was looking for.

"What did Jason poison you with?"

"Look for *ryana* serum."

Nothing. "What else?"

Pointless. Let me die. "It doesn't—"

"What . . . else!"

"I don't know!"

With no more time to lose, he grabbed fistfuls of vials and stuffed his pockets to capacity. "I've grabbed what I can. Pray there's something in there Doc can find useful. Let's go."

He half dragged Faolan to the emergency escape hatch, pausing long enough to use his code to trigger the alarms for the building.

"That will be heard from the street and will release all the locks. Should cause enough of a distraction to get us out."

"Can't run fast." Faolan's words slurred as he spoke. "You go—"

"Old conversation, already dealt with. Move, Wolf."

It took all his strength to push Faolan out the small escape door in the back alley, then into the throng of people milling around the marketplace by the guild building. Weak fingers gripped his biceps as they moved, Faolan barely able to maintain his hold. Gar looped an arm securely around Faolan's waist and pulled him tight against his side.

"You're not going anywhere. I'm not leaving you behind, and there is no way in hell you're dying. Do you understand me? So keep moving those feet of yours."

Love you.

The thought flashed through his mind so fast, Gar wasn't sure he'd heard it. *Gods, not him too. I can't lose Faolan and be left all alone.* There was no time for an interrogation, so he kept moving forward until they reached the edge of the city.

"See, Wolf. No one chasing us and we're clear of the city. Just a bit farther to the ship."

"Slave driver." Faolan held on a bit tighter.

"Don't forget it."

They didn't stop until they reached the tree line. Faolan threw his body against the first secluded trunk he could reach, bracing his back against the thick wood. Gar took in his pale complexion, not at all liking the way his body trembled or the glassy look of his eyes.

"I think you have a concussion."

"Nearly got my head blown off, so it's not—"

Faolan's sentence died in his mouth as his eyes grew wide, fixed on a point behind Gar. Gar didn't need to turn around to know they'd been followed by another bounty hunter. He could hear the blaster engage as it was powered to full.

"Turn around." The voice was familiar.

Gar held his hands up and moved to shield Faolan with his body. "Byron."

The only hunter Gar considered even remotely close to a friend stood before him with a blaster pointed directly at his chest. There was no way Gar would be able to pull his own weapon up to get a shot off before Byron killed him, and Faolan was in no shape to defend anyone.

"When the word came out Jason put a bounty on your head, I couldn't believe it. Then I saw you and that one leaving the guild, and I knew something was up."

Get out of here, Gar. He'll take me and leave if you offer.

He had one chance to play this right. Keeping as still as possible, Gar ignored Faolan.

"Jason's dead. He killed my parents years ago, and thought I'd find out the truth from Faolan here."

Byron frowned. "Faolan?"

Shit. First rule of the guild—don't get too close to your mark. "Yes, Faolan. He's . . . We're friends."

"You know better than that, Stitt." His tone was harsh, but Byron eased up on his blaster.

"I know . . . I really don't care. Faolan has shown me more . . . Just let us go. Please."

Faolan's soft gasp followed by the gentle hand on Gar's shoulder told him the sentiment wasn't lost. Byron's gaze drifted from Gar's face to the contact between them.

Byron shook his head and replaced his blaster in his holster. "I'll be damned. The Ice Man thawed."

Gar stiffened, but Faolan tugged on him. "The nice man is letting us escape. Time to go."

The realization nearly passed him by until Faolan's gentle *Take me home* brushed across his mind. Gar reached up to cover Faolan's hand, nodding to Byron. "Thank you."

"Don't come back to the guild. If Jason is gone, then someone will need to take over. And I'll lose my shot at it if anyone finds out I let you and Wolf go."

"Can't think of a better man for the job. Thanks, Byron."

"Go."

This time it was Faolan who held *him* as they made their way back to the ship.

CHAPTER
SEVENTEEN

Faolan wasn't ready to admit he'd grown to care for the man standing in front of him—especially since the man in question was being a complete ass at the moment.

"Are you absolutely sure?" Gar's eyes had grown impossibly wide. He hadn't let go of some part of Faolan's body since arriving back on the *Belle Kurve*, but anything resembling a conversation had been less than forthcoming. "I mean those could be anything. The chances I'd actually grab something useful . . ."

Doc had been shocked at the meds Gar had thrown onto the exam table beside Faolan, and the hurried explanation as to why they were important. Faolan hadn't been coherent enough at the time to appreciate exactly what his lover had grabbed before hauling his ass out of the guild, or the significance of what he'd said to Doc.

His secret was out.

"Mr. Stitt, if you're going to refuse to listen to me, then you can get the hell out of my med bay. Do I make myself clear? I've helped with the concussion, now let me do the rest of my job."

Faolan knew he should be reacting with joy, or at the very least cracking a smile at the news, but he couldn't quite bring himself to do so.

Gar had, completely at random, grabbed three vials of a drug used to treat *ryana* poisoning. Not a cure, but close enough.

Doc hadn't been pleased when Gar spilled the facts of Faolan's condition to her. She'd yelled at Faolan for a solid ten minutes as to why he hadn't told her the second he'd become ill, then pulled him into a crushing hug, then started running a full bio scan. He knew

Gar heard every curse floating through his head—he had yet to take the stone off.

"With this I can squeeze in another good five to ten years for you."

Five to ten years—it was five to ten more than he'd expected. Swallowing, he tried to keep his head clear of any thoughts as he let the new information sink in. "As long as the bounty hunters don't get me first."

Doc chuckled. "Well, no one claimed piracy against the Loyalists garnered a long life. It's better than the three months you had."

Gar sucked in a breath as a jolt hit Faolan's body. "So little?"

"The meds you took masked the symptoms, but did very little to stall the poison. You're lucky to be alive at all."

He should be dead—the realization scared the shit out of him.

"Doc, would you mind administering a dose now?" Gar asked after a moment of silence, his hand sliding along the back of Faolan's neck. "I'll take him to his quarters after that and force him to rest."

Faolan saw the silent look traded between Gar and the doctor. Instead of ignoring it, he slid off the bed and crossed his arms. "Doc, shoot me up with that stuff and let me get back to my quarters. Stitt and I need to talk."

Smirk on her face, Doc nodded as she prepared the injection. "Who am I to stand in the way of a couple's spat?"

"We're not a couple," Faolan said at the same time as Gar.

Doc tried to hide her smile, to no avail. "Of course not. Now don't move, Captain. This is going to sting."

The serum didn't sting—it burned, twisting through his circulatory system. Faolan cried out, his legs weakening as the poison fought against its attacker. Before he fell to the floor, Gar's strong arms caught him and held him up.

"Shit. Get him on the bed, Stitt."

"No." Faolan pushed Doc away. "My quarters."

"Are you an idiot? This was way further advanced than I realized. You're not going anywhere without medical supervision." Doc shoved a strand of her red hair behind her ear. "No arguing."

Gods, I don't want anyone to see me like this. "Last time I checked, Doc, I was still captain of this ship."

"I'll keep an eye on him." Gar's deep voice cut through the tension. "If there's a problem, I'll let you know."

Doc let out a short huff. "If there's a problem, I doubt he'll let *you* know."

"Don't worry about it. I have ways of making him talk." Gar pulled Faolan close. "Come on, Captain. Let's get you to your bed before your crew realizes you're a mere mortal."

"I can walk." Faolan stepped away from him. "Let's just get there fast."

The halls of the ship were busy as always. But as they walked toward his quarters, Gar's body too close to be casual, Faolan's annoyance grew steadily.

"I'm not a child you need to hover over, Stitt."

"You say I'm stubborn." Gar spoke only loud enough for Faolan to hear.

Still, he backed off half a pace, making it easier for Faolan to get his bearings. There was something about Gar, the scent of his body, the strength of his touch—all of it drove Faolan to distraction.

Ignoring the questioning looks of his crew as they passed, they finally reached his quarters with only minor difficulty. The moment the door slid closed behind them, Faolan's body trembled, and he fell to his knees.

"You really are an idiot, Wolf."

This isn't fair. "I never said I wasn't."

Gar pulled him up and manhandled him to sit on the edge of his bed. "What isn't fair?"

Gods-damn stone. "Take that fucking thing off, will you?"

"I will when you start talking to me." Gar dropped to his knees between Faolan's legs. Large hands rubbed up Faolan's thighs, easing away the pain. "You're hurt and scared."

Faolan looked away. "Freaked out a bit. Not scared."

"Fine. Regardless, you're not alone in all this. Let me help."

You won't stay. The thought flashed through Faolan's mind before he could stop it. He knew Gar heard by the way he flinched.

"Why would you think that?" Gar squeezed his thighs.

"You don't owe me anything, Stitt. We had a little adventure together, some great sex, a couple of laughs. It's not like I'm expecting you to give up your life and become a pirate. You already said you prefer to be on your own." *So lonely.*

Faolan knew he was being a coward, and turned back to face Gar. What he saw in his expression shocked him. Blue eyes were wide and red-rimmed. His full lips were parted as his tongue darted out to wet them. Gar looked like a man on the edge of making a very large decision—Faolan prayed he'd like the outcome.

They stared at each other for a long time. Faolan didn't know if Gar was picking up on his thoughts or if he was lost in his own. Gar sat back on his heels, slowly reached up, and undid the chain that held the stone around his neck. Instead of putting it in Faolan's hand, he clasped it around his neck.

"I think it's only fair you hear what's going on in my head, since I've had a front seat to your thoughts." Gar loosened the knot of his tie and undid the top two buttons of his shirt.

Faolan hadn't read Gar before. He was expecting the same confused numbness he'd experienced when he'd connected to Mace. There was none of that. The low buzz morphed into a full-out rush of heat as Gar's thoughts jumped into his head.

Want to be with you.

Faolan froze. He was scared that if he moved, breathed, then whatever it was Gar wanted to say to him would never come out. Gar looked just as nervous, his fingers rubbing the bottom of his tie.

"Since I saw my dad die and thought Mace had been killed because of me, I made a point of keeping my distance from other people. I didn't think I could . . . handle it if someone else I cared about . . . well, if something happened to them." *Broke me.*

Faolan leaned forward and pulled Gar into a tight embrace as he thought of Kayla. "I know."

Gar turned, pressing a kiss to Faolan's neck. "I thought I could go my whole life and not need to feel any sort of connection. I know that's not the case."

"I'm glad. No one should spend their life alone."

"Not even if that individual is surrounded by people?"

Before Faolan could answer, Gar rose to his feet and pushed him back so he was lying flat on his back. Gar held him still by the weight of his gaze.

"Gar?"

"I've watched you with everyone. I don't know if it's the responsibility of command or if you're just as scared of getting burned, but you're as alone as me. You smile and laugh and talk without ever telling anyone what you really feel. You can't hide from me, Faolan. I've been in your head, seen the type of man you really are."

Faolan couldn't even manage a fake smile. "What kind of man am I?"

"Loyal. Brave. You care more about people than you'd ever say. Stubborn." *Loving.*

"I'll give you stubborn." He struggled to sit up, but Gar shook his head.

"You need to rest. You mothered me for a week, I can do the same to you." *We can do things* for each other. *I'm not alone anymore.*

"None of this is what you wanted to tell me." Faolan didn't need the stone to know that much.

Gar fidgeted with his shirt sleeves, his eyes glancing around the room. "I know you don't do . . . this. And I find myself going into uncharted space."

"What do you mean?"

"I want to stay on the *Belle Kurve*." *I want to stay with you. I love—* "I don't need to tell you what I feel. I mean, the stone should have shown you."

Faolan raised a hand and beckoned, drawing Gar down to lie next to him on the bed, rolling to his side so they faced one another. When their eyes met, Faolan reached up and jerked the chain so the stone fell free of his neck. Setting it between their bodies on the mattress, he laced their fingers together.

"I'd like that. If you stayed."

Gar's lips twitched into a soft smile. "Can you spare the quarters, Captain?"

Faolan frowned at the mattress. "We'll have to move your bed in here from the *Geilt*. It's more comfortable."

Gar rolled his eyes. "You're just using me for my possessions."

"As any good pirate would."

"Are you sure?"

Faolan reached down and grabbed Gar's cock. "Did you suddenly turn into a girl on me?"

"Fuck off."

Faolan kissed him with a final nip on Gar's bottom lip. "Come live with us. Get to know your sister. Help make my last five to ten years happy."

"I'll help you find a cure, then we can have *more* than ten years." The light in Gar's eyes flared bright, aimed directly at Faolan. "How have you come to mean so much to me in such a short time?"

"Never question the heart, Gar. We just go along for the ride."

"Faolan, I think that . . . I mean I feel like I . . ."

His heart constricted, and that same mind-blowing awe Kayla had brought out in him hit Faolan full force in the chest. It was too soon to say the words—scared the vocalization would cheapen the power of his emotions. Doing the only thing he could think of, Faolan moved their joined hands to where the stone lay. Parting their palms enough to let the stone rest between them, he kissed Gar's shoulder, waiting a heartbeat before thinking as clearly as he could. *I love you too.*

Explore the rest of the *Bounty* series:
www.riptidepublishing.com/titles/series/bounty

Dear Reader,

Thank you for reading Christine d'Abo's *No Quarter*!

We know your time is precious and you have many, many entertainment options, so it means a lot that you've chosen to spend your time reading. We really hope you enjoyed it.

We'd be honored if you'd consider posting a review—good or bad—on sites like **Amazon, Barnes & Noble, Kobo, Goodreads, Twitter, Facebook**, **Tumblr**, and your blog or website. We'd also be honored if you told your friends and family about this book. Word of mouth is a book's lifeblood!

For more information on upcoming releases, author interviews, blog tours, contests, giveaways, and more, please sign up for our weekly, spam-free newsletter and visit us around the web:

Newsletter: tinyurl.com/RiptideSignup
Twitter: twitter.com/RiptideBooks
Facebook: facebook.com/RiptidePublishing
Goodreads: tinyurl.com/RiptideOnGoodreads
Tumblr: riptidepublishing.tumblr.com

Thank you so much for Reading the Rainbow!

RiptidePublishing.com

ABOUT THE

AUTHOR

A romance novelist and short story writer, Christine has over thirty publications to her name. She loves to exercise and stops writing just long enough to keep her body in motion too. When she's not pretending to be a ninja in her basement, she's most likely spending time with her family and two dogs.

Website: www.christinedabo.com
Twitter: @Christine_dAbo
Facebook: facebook.com/christine.dabo
Instagram: instagram.com/christine.dabo
Tumblr: christinedabo.tumblr.com

Enjoy more stories like
No Quarter
at RiptidePublishing.com!

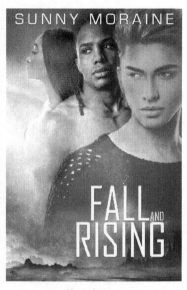